I0623003

Highland Redemption

A Duncurra Legacy Novel

By
Ceci Giltenan

This is a work of fiction. The characters, incidents, locations and dialogues in this book are of the author's imagination and are not to be construed as real. Any resemblance to actual events or persons, living or dead, is completely coincidental. Any actual locations mentioned in this book are used fictitiously.

No part of this book may be reproduced or transmitted in any form or by any means, electronic or mechanical, including photocopying, recording, or by any information storage and retrieval system, without permission in writing from the author.

All rights are retained by the author. No part of this book may be reproduced or transmitted in any form or by any means, electronic or mechanical, including photocopying, recording, or by any information storage and retrieval system, without permission in writing from the publisher except in the case of brief quotations embodied in critical articles or reviews. The unauthorized reproduction, sharing, or distribution of this copyrighted work is illegal. Criminal copyright infringement, including infringement without monetary gain, is investigated by the FBI and is punishable by up to five years in federal prison and a fine of $250,000.

Copyright 2017 by Ceci Giltenan
www.duncurra.com

Cover Design: Earthly Charms

ISBN-10: 1-942623-60-7
ISBN-13: 978-1-942623-60-1

Produced in the USA

DEDICATION

To Barbara, you are stronger and braver than any Highland warrior I could ever imagine.

To Lily and Kathryn, you raise me up.

And, to my beloved husband, Eamon. I couldn't do this without you.

ACKNOWLEDGEMENTS

I owe a huge thank you to my all my beta readers, especially Virginia, Susan, Sarah, Patricia, Melz, Lisa, Kathryn, Eileen, Dharti, Ann, Annie, Annie and April, who provided early feedback. This book is better because of you.

A special thanks to beta reader Shannon Leupp who provided some interesting historical background about the Hanseatic League.

"Darkness cannot drive out darkness; only light can do that. Hate cannot drive out hate, only love can do that."

~ Martin Luther King Jr.,
"Love Your Enemies" Sermon (1957)

PROLOGUE

Cotharach Castle, Clan Ruthven
January 26, 1367

Ambrose Ruthven knelt by the bed, holding his wife's hand. Moibeal had drawn her last breath earlier that morning, but he hadn't been able to leave her. Somehow, to release her hand would be to let her go, and he wasn't ready for that— he'd never be ready for that. They hadn't had enough time. Seven years was not nearly enough time. He relived memory after memory, unwilling to accept that they were all he had left.

He remembered when he'd first met Moibeal.

He'd gone to court, representing Clan Ruthven for his brother, Ainsley, Laird Ruthven.

"While you're there, find yourself a bride, brother," Ainsley told him.

Twenty-eight at the time, Ambrose hoped to do just that, to find a suitable wife among the courtiers. Ainsley had given Ambrose a list of clans with which he would like to forge a closer bond.

But Ainsley, having lost his own wife three years earlier, had become sentimental. "Life is short, brother, too short. An alliance with one of these families would be ideal, but if you meet a lass who pleases you, I'll see what I can do."

At the time, Ambrose thought his brother was a fool. Ambrose would certainly look for a wife, but as a second son, he wanted a wealthy wife or one that would bring him a title. That was until he'd met Moibeal Dundas. Clan Dundas was not on Ainsley's list. Neither were they exceedingly wealthy and, as the daughter of the laird's youngest brother, Moibeal didn't hold a title.

But she instantly held Ambrose's heart. She took his breath away. She had a soft curvaceous figure, thick chestnut-colored hair, and green eyes that always seemed to be filled with laughter. At eighteen, she was ten years his junior. Still, as noble marriages went, that was no real difference at all. He had been completely smitten with her and to his delight, she seemed fond of him too.

So, true to his word, Ainsley contacted Laird Dundas requesting a meeting to discuss a betrothal. Laird Dundas travelled to Cotharach with Moibeal and her parents. When they arrived, they'd seemed happy and open to the prospect of a marriage. Ainsley had greeted them with a grand feast and at the end of the evening, everyone was in high spirits. Ambrose believed that by the next day, he would be betrothed to the woman he adored.

But that didn't happen. Laird Dundas had misunderstood Ainsley's request. He thought Ainsley himself was seeking her hand, which would have made Moibeal Lady Ruthven. Ainsley had explained that he still mourned his late wife. He was not ready to marry now, and perhaps never would be.

However, absolutely certain he would never marry again, Ainsley made Laird Dundas an offer so generous, it had utterly astounded Ambrose at the time. "Laird Dundas, I only have a daughter and as I don't intend to marry again, it is unlikely I'll ever have a son. I will stipulate that if Ambrose and Moibeal do have a son, my title will pass to Ambrose, and then his son. Even without a title, though, as you are well aware, my brother is a wealthy man in his own right. He has built an extremely successful shipping business and would be an excellent husband for Moibeal."

Laird Dundas wanted none of it. He believed that in a few years, Ainsley's grief would ease, he would take a wife, and could possibly have a son of his own then. He didn't care that Ambrose was wealthy. The only betrothal the laird would consider was one with Ainsley.

And that was that. They left, taking with them Ambrose's hopes of happiness.

Moibeal was married to Raghnall Napier, Laird Napier's heir, just after Epiphany. And as if fate were laughing at Ambrose, Ainsley died less than a month later, making Katherine, Ainsley's thirteen-year-old daughter, Lady Ruthven. Ambrose would only *act* as Laird on her behalf, the title of Laird Ruthven ultimately going to whomever she married. Ambrose inherited all of the headaches with none of the benefits.

After that, whenever he saw Moibeal, his heart ached and jealousy for Raghnall Napier burned in his gut. Worse, the laughter in her eyes had been replaced by same wistful longing he suspected was in his own gaze. Seeing her miserable tore at his heart.

Ambrose became angry and bitter. Eventually, he realized the only way he would ever benefit from the mess destiny had dealt him was if his niece never married. At least then he would become Laird Ruthven. So, ensuring that eventuality became his goal.

Finally, a few years later, fate took a turn in his favor. Moibeal became a widow. Raghnall and, tragically, their young son, both succumbed to illness. Ambrose had another chance at happiness, but only if he could wrest full leadership of the clan from Katherine's hands. He redoubled his efforts, even seeking the aid of King David II. By some miracle, the king found a husband for Katherine, Niall MacIan, who would renounce her titles and lands. MacIan was the laird of an impoverished Highland clan, with a title and lands of his own, but desperately in need of funds.

Ambrose had finally been able to marry the heart of his heart mere months after his niece had been packed off to the Highlands. So grateful was he to his king, Ambrose had vowed to name their first child David.

He smiled at the memory as he gripped her cold hand tighter. "Do you remember that, my love? I was certain you were carrying a lad. You actually laughed the first time I held the wee sprite. I had to settle for naming her Davida."

He could almost hear the laughter that had delighted him so. "It wasn't enough time, my love. We were supposed to grow old together. How can I let you go?" His voice broke on a sob and he finally gave into the tears he'd been fighting for hours. How could he possibly continue on without her?

The door to the chamber opened and Ambrose whirled around to roar at whomever dared disturb him, but the chastisement died on his lips. It was his lovely six-year-old daughter, Davida.

"Papa? Are you still saying goodbye to mama?"

"Aye, Vida."

"Can I come in?"

"Aye, my wee darling."

She slipped quietly into the room and crossed to his side. He put one arm around her and kissed the top of her head. She wrapped both her small arms around him, rested her cheek on his chest, and looked at her mother. "Mama was very pretty, wasn't she?"

"Aye," he choked on a sob. "Aye, she was."

"I loved mama and mama loved us. She said she did."

Ambrose trembled, unable to do anything but nod.

"But you know what else she said, Papa?"

"What else did she say, precious?"

"She said she didn't want to go, but she had to leave us and not to worry about her because she would be with the angels. I asked her if I could go with her and she said no. She said you needed me to stay here and be your angel."

Of course, she would have said that. He could almost hear her now, telling him, "You must go on, my love. You must go on for Vida. It's time to let me go now."

He sighed heavily and, letting go of Moibeal's hand, wrapped both arms around his daughter, the living, breathing angel his wife had given him. "That's right, Vida. Mama is with the angels, but we have each other."

He stood, lifting Vida as he did. He walked with her to the door, turning to look back one last time. "Goodbye, my love. I will miss you."

CHAPTER 1

October 4, 1378
On the road, north of Perth

It was a clear, crisp evening and the moon was bright enough to illumine the road ahead of them, for which Tomas MacIan was thankful. This was their second day of travel and with the light of the moon, they could ride for several more hours before stopping for the night. The journey from Edinburgh to Duncurra could take up to seven days this time of the year, so the longer they rode tonight, the better.

He was never happier to be on the way home to Duncurra, than when he was leaving the royal court. At twenty-six, he had attended court several times before, but he never enjoyed it. The ride home was always his favorite part. This trip, like the others, had been to deliver the taxes Clan MacIan owed the crown. However, Laird Niall MacIan, the man who had adopted Tomas over nineteen years ago, usually made the journey too. This time he hadn't and Tomas was the official representative for Clan MacIan.

But because transporting large sums of money was always risky, they usually made the trip together with representatives from other, closely allied clans. This year Clan Carr and Clan MacLennan rode with them. Altogether, they were a band of eighteen well-trained warriors and much too great a force to be set upon by thieves. Of course, on the road home there was less fear of that, as the taxes had been paid and they didn't carry a significant amount of gold.

Laird Carr, who by virtue of his rank was the group's leader, slowed his horse and held up a hand signaling silence.

When their own company grew quiet, Tomas heard men yelling and the clanging of swords from somewhere ahead of them.

Laird Carr frowned. "Someone's been set upon by highwaymen, likely at the crossroads ahead. We'll lend our aid." He drew his sword and kicked his horse into a gallop, motioning for them to follow.

They reached the crossroads in a minute, and sure enough, about a half of a mile down the road leading west, a carriage had been waylaid by a band of thieves. As the Highlanders rode hard towards them, Tomas surveyed the scene.

The men guarding the coach were not only outnumbered, but they had inferior skills. A nobleman, evidently one of the carriage occupants, stood fighting a bandit at one entrance, even as another of the miscreants entered the other side, pulling a woman from it. She screamed and fought until the man backhanded her hard enough to stun her. Before she recovered, he had her on the back of a horse, riding away from the scene.

Tomas became furious. Seeing one of them strike a woman was enough to confirm for him who the villains were. When they reached the carriage, he skirted the battling men and continued racing down the road after the pair.

The kidnapper, riding double on a poorer mount, was easy to catch. Perhaps realizing it was his only hope of success, the man shoved the lass off the horse, drew his sword, and turned to fight Tomas.

"Ye've already lost this battle, man," said Tomas. "Throw down yer weapon."

"I don't think I will," said the man, brandishing his sword, ready for a fight.

Tomas was deadly with a sword. He'd been trained by his uncle Fingal, who was one of the best swordsmen in the Highlands. Tomas would give the man one more chance. "This is yer last warning. Surrender, or die."

"Not today. That prize is worth fighting for and I suspect I can best a Highland pup."

It was the last mistake the highwayman ever made.

Tomas cut him down in mere moments. Then he immediately turned his attention to the woman who had moved off the road into the trees. She stood, holding on to a tree trunk for dear life. On closer inspection, Tomas realized "woman" was a bit of an exaggeration. She was young, no older than his sister Beitris who had just turned eighteen.

Tomas jumped off his mount and strode toward her. "Are ye hurt, lass?"

Her eyes were wide and frightened. She shook her head, stumbling backwards a step.

Not wishing to scare her more, he stopped several paces away from her. "Ye've nothing to fear. I'll not harm ye." He held his hand out to her. "Come then, I'll take ye back to yer carriage. I suspect the other thieves have been dealt with."

She looked at him warily for a moment, then took a step toward him and winced.

"Ye are hurt."

"Aye. A little. I hurt my ankle when I hit the ground after he shoved me off the horse."

"I'll carry ye then." Before she could object, he had closed the distance between them and lifted her into his arms. She was small and delicate and smelled of roses. He carried her to his great black warhorse, Duff. "Steady now, lad, we have a precious cargo."

He lifted her onto the beast's back and mounted behind her. "I'm going to put an arm around ye, to steady ye, lass."

She nodded before casting a sidelong glance at the dead highwayman. She shuddered and looked away.

Tomas clicked to Duff. Better just to get her away from here.

As they approached the carriage, the scene was no better. The thieves all lay dead. Most of the men who had been guarding the carriage were injured. But none of the Highlanders traveling with Tomas had so much as a scratch.

They were patching up the wounded and dragging the dead off the road.

When the nobleman saw Tomas approach, he ran towards them.

"My precious lass. Thank God, you're safe." He lifted her down.

"Papa," she cried, wrapping her arms around him.

He kissed her forehead tenderly. Then, turning to look up at Tomas, said, "Thank you, sir. I am forever in your debt for saving my daughter."

The moon illuminated the man's face and Tomas's blood chilled. It was *Ambrose Ruthven*, his adoptive mother's uncle and the man who had nearly beaten her to death over nineteen years ago. Tomas's back also bore the scars of Ruthven's whip.

"Who are you, lad?" Ruthven asked.

Tomas was not about to tell Ambrose Ruthven who he really was. He answered "Sir Tomas…MacHenry."

The other men who traveled with him gave him surprised looks. Well, it wasn't totally untrue. Tomas's natural father and grandfather were both named Henry. But Ruthven didn't need to know that. Ruthven also didn't need to know that both men had worked in the stables at Cotharach Castle their whole lives, as had Tomas until the age of seven.

"Thank you, Sir Tomas. I'm Laird Ambrose Ruthven, and this is my daughter, Lady Vida." He turned towards the other men. "I owe you all a great debt. How is it you happened to be on the road this night?"

Laird Carr answered. "We have been at the royal court and are returning home to the Highlands. I'm Hugh Carr, Laird of Clan Carr. This is my son, Edward."

Edward gave a small bow.

Laird Carr made no other introductions. "I believe we aren't far from Ruthven territory. Some of my men will escort ye there while the rest of us bury the dead. Then we'll continue on our way home."

"Thank ye, Laird Carr, I'm in your debt. Please, allow me to offer you the hospitality of Cotharach Castle before you continue your journey."

Tomas went rigid. *Say, no. Please say no.*

"That's very kind of ye, Laird Ruthven, but ye should get your daughter home while the moon is bright. There's still work to be done here."

Tomas breathed a sigh of relief.

Ruthven waved away the objection. "You needn't worry about these miscreants. I'll send men back tomorrow with a wagon and have them deliver the bodies to the Lord Sheriff in Perth. We'll bring their horses with us."

Laird Carr looked as if he were about to refuse again, when the lass added her voice. "Please, Laird Carr, it is the very least we can do. Allow us to extend our hospitality…even if only for one night."

Laird Carr sighed. "Aye. For one night, then. Thank ye."

Damnation. Cotharach Castle was the last place on earth Tomas wanted to go, but now there was no avoiding it now. Still, in Laird Carr's defense, Tomas wasn't sure he could have looked into those beautiful, entreating eyes and said no.

Ruthven helped his daughter to the carriage, his men tethered the thieves' horses, and then everyone mounted up.

Laird Carr sent several of the men-at-arms who accompanied them to ride in front of the carriage with the Ruthven men.

Then he motioned for Tomas and the remainder of their party to fall in behind the carriage and maneuvered his way close to Tomas. The MacIan guardsman who had accompanied them, his good friend Ethan MacLeod, and one of his father's captains, Rowan MacKenzie, did the same.

Laird MacLennan, who hated going to the royal court, had sent his right hand, the captain of his guard, Quinn MacKenzie, to represent him. Quinn and Rowan were brothers. Accompanying Quinn were two MacLennan guardsmen, Kieran and Drew MacBain. The MacBains were cousins of some sort and Drew was perhaps Tomas's closest friends. They'd trained together under Laird MacLennan. He was well acquainted with Kieran, too. His father was a MacLennan guardsman, and Kieran had trained at Duncurra.

When they had dropped back far enough so as not to be overheard, Laird Carr addressed Tomas. "I'm assuming ye lied about who ye were because ye recognized him. Is that Lady Katherine's uncle? The one who traded her hand and money for her title?"

"Aye, Laird. And who nearly killed her with his whip. You've heard the story. I was the stable boy at Cotharach then. Ruthven became furious with me because I tried to tend a horse he'd ridden too hard before cleaning his saddle. He started beating me with his whip and she put herself between us to protect me, so he beat her instead." Tomas had felt guilty about that his whole life.

Kieran frowned. "But your back is scarred too. Is he the one who did it?"

"Aye, on other occasions. He had a foul temper and was quick to use the whip."

"By all that's holy," swore Rowan, "If yer da were here, Ruthven would be a dead man."

"If yer uncle were here, he'd be a dead man," added Quinn.

"No, he wouldn't," countered Laird Carr. "Because like it or not, had Ruthven not bartered Katherine and her fortune for her title, Niall wouldn't have her as his wife. Besides, ye know for certain, he wouldn't have wanted that lass harmed."

Tomas couldn't argue with Laird Carr. Truthfully, for years, Da's fondest desire, as well as that of Uncle Fingal, and all of the guardsmen who had accompanied them on that trip, had been to extract their pound of flesh from the bastard. Nevertheless, none would ever have acted on it. Everything had worked out for the best in spite of Ambrose Ruthven.

"So," added Laird Carr, "Since ye obviously thought it better not to identify yerself as a MacIan, we'll keep the secret. For that matter, he doesn't need to know MacLennans ride with us either. They are well-known as yer da's closest allies. Until we leave Ruthven land, ye're all *my* clansmen. See that everyone knows that."

"Is there a chance ye'll be recognized by any of the Ruthven clan members once we reach Cotharach?" asked Ethan, who'd first met Tomas when they were both fourteen.

Rowan laughed. "Not likely. He was a scrawny wee thing until he was about twelve or thirteen."

Tomas chuckled too. "Even then I was all arms and legs and feet. It took a few years to fill out." But he had filled out. At just under six feet, he wasn't quite as tall as his adoptive father or uncle, but he was every bit as broad shouldered and strong. "Nay, I have to agree with Rowan, no one is likely to peg me as the stable boy who ran away years ago. I don't expect anyone even remembers me."

Nothing more was said about it as they rode another hour to reach Ruthven's home.

The moon was high and, if possible, even brighter as they approached Cotharach's village. Cotharach, a timber castle surrounded by a spiked wooden palisade, stood on the banks of Loch Abaid. Everything looked smaller than he'd remembered but little had changed.

By the time they'd ridden through the village, the gates had been opened to them.

Laird Ruthven alighted from his carriage and called orders to castle servants and stable hands.

"My men will see to your mounts, Laird Carr."

"That's kind of ye, Laird Ruthven, but there are so many of us, we'll make quick work of it if we tend our horses ourselves."

"Whatever ye wish. This is Manus, my steward," said Ruthven, indicating an older man standing to one side. "He'll see that ye have what ye need, then show ye into the hall. My daughter sustained a few minor injuries. I'll just see to her and join ye shortly."

He turned back to the carriage and assisted her out. She clung to her father's arm and winced as he helped her hobble toward the keep.

Tomas couldn't stand to see her in pain. "Excuse me, Laird. I know Lady Vida's ankle is injured and it's clearly paining her. I can carry her into the keep, if ye wish."

Ambrose beamed at him. "Thank you, Sir Tomas, I would appreciate that."

Tomas lifted her into his arms and looked into her eyes. To his relief, the fear he'd seen earlier was gone.

She smiled at him. "Aye, thank you, Sir Tomas."

He followed her father up the stairs to the keep. The doors opened to an entryway from which double doors stood open, revealing the flurry of activity in the great hall. To his surprise, Tomas recognized a few of the people working there. Moyna, who had been in charge of the kitchen when he was a lad, had aged quite a bit but still seemed spry and efficient. She was calling orders, seeing that tables were set up and food laid out.

A woman about his mother's age came rushing toward them. It was Emma, the girl who had served as Katherine's maid, and for a moment Tomas feared she'd recognized him.

But her attention was solely on Vida. "Oh, my lady, what happened?"

"It's a long story, Emma, but I'll tell you everything later."

"Bring her this way," said Laird Ruthven, heading towards the stairs.

Tomas followed the Laird and his heart lurched when Ruthven led them to his mother's old bedchamber. The difference in the room reminded him of just how badly she'd been treated by her uncle. No longer sparsely furnished, now it looked the way a noblewoman's chamber should look. The threadbare hangings and counterpane had been replaced with elegant silk brocade and velvet. Plush rugs covered the floor. Thick draperies hung over the windows to keep out the chill. A huge wardrobe stood against one wall. Its door was ajar, revealing dozens of beautiful garments.

"Put her here on the bed," said Ambrose.

Tomas placed her on it gently as Emma propped pillows behind her.

Vida laid a hand on his arm as he stepped away. "Thank you, Sir Tomas. Thank you for everything."

He was momentarily lost in her green eyes. "Ye're very welcome, my lady. I hope yer ankle is feeling better soon." He gave a small bow. Then to Laird Ruthven he said, "Please excuse me, Laird. I'll just go see to my mount now."

"Certainly, Sir Tomas. You have my thanks as well."

Tomas left the room and fairly ran down the stairs and out of the keep. The sooner he was away from Cotharach, the better. He didn't like the memories.

When he reached the stable, most of the men had finished tending their beasts and were ready for a meal and a good night's sleep. Ethan, Kieran, Drew, and Edward waited for him.

"So, what's the whole story?" asked Drew as Tomas removed Duff's saddle and rubbed the horse down.

Tomas glanced around to see that no Ruthven servants remained within hearing. "You know I'm adopted. Edward, you might remember when it happened."

"I remember when Laird MacIan came back from the lowlands with Lady Katherine. She had a gray mare she

22

called Stormy that he didn't think was fit for the journey so he gave it to my da, who gave it to my oldest sister. But it was some time after that when we heard they'd adopted ye."

"And, I knew the Laird had adopted ye," said Ethan, "but I'd always assumed ye were a MacIan clansman. I didn't know ye'd been the stable boy here."

Kieran's jaw dropped.

Drew laughed. "Ye're jesting. Ye weren't really a lowland stable boy."

"'Tis no jest. I was. When Laird MacIan arrived here with orders from the king that Lady Katherine should marry him, she told me to take the northwest road from the village and wait there in the trees so I could go with her. She had always been kind to me and her Uncle Ambrose was a cruel bastard. She was worried about what might happen to me when she left."

"Well, this is rich," said Kieran. "That *cruel bastard* now owes his former stable boy a huge debt."

"Perhaps, but I just want to get the hell out of here as soon as the sun's up. I left this life behind and I want nothing more to do with it."

CHAPTER 2

This had been the day from hell for Ambrose Ruthven. Had it not been for Laird Carr and his men…he shuddered to think of how much worse it could have been. After Vida was settled, he played host to them until they were bedded down for the night. Then he retreated to his solar and poured himself a glass of whisky.

He was between the proverbial rock and hard place. When he became Laird Ruthven, he'd owned a fledging shipping business that, from the start, was much more profitable than the Ruthven holding, so that was where he put his time and effort. As long as the land was at least modestly profitable and no one starved, he was happy.

In the last ten years, his business had burgeoned. The huge guilds that had dominated the shipping industry in northern Europe, known as the Hanseatic League, were in disarray. Outbreaks of the plague in Europe had claimed the lives of a large number of sailors. It opened the door for smaller merchants from England, Scotland, and Ireland to seize a larger portion of the market.

Thus, the bulk of his shipping business involved trade with northern Europe and the Baltics, along the Hanseatic routes. However, he knew the real wealth came from the Mediterranean. Over the last few years, he'd seen several men turn huge profits sailing to ports in Spain and Italy. However, in the amount of time it took for a single ship to sail to and return from Italy once, the same ship could have made four trips to Baltic ports. On the other hand, the profit from one ship returning from the Mediterranean was ten times what could be earned from trade with northern Europe. As with everything, the greater the profit, the greater the risk. Not only were the voyages longer, they were more dangerous and required a major financial investment up front. It could take anywhere from four to six months for a ship to sail to Genoa and return and even longer for a ship bound to Venice.

Although worried about the risks, he had toyed with the idea for ages. Finally in late June, he'd made the investment. He had sent one of his ten ships, the *Mermaid Queen,* to Genoa. Then in July, he sent the *Merry Mistress* to Venice. It tied up a huge amount of his funds, but he believed it would pay off.

In fact, he was so confident that when he incurred a large gambling debt to Naughton Lindsay, a younger brother of Laird Lindsay, he'd secured the debt with his Genoa shipment.

"You know I'm good for it, Naughton. When that ship returns, it'll bring four times what I owe you, or more."

Naughton had agreed. "Yes, I've found my Mediterranean-bound ships to be golden. The increased risk is worth the enormous profit. I'm sure you're good for it. And never fear, if something goes awry, you can give me your daughter's hand in marriage instead."

Everyone at the table that night had laughed about it, including Ambrose. He had no intention of giving Vida in marriage to Naughton Lindsay. Thankfully, it wouldn't be necessary.

He incurred the debt because he was certain he could repay it. Just before Michaelmas, Naughton inquired about what Ambrose's intentions were regarding repayment. Ambrose responded by saying Clan Ruthven was in the midst of the harvest. He would visit his shipping office in Dundee very soon and would know more then.

That's where he and Vida had been earlier in the week. Unfortunately, there had been no word of either ship.

To make matters worse, while in Dundee, Lindsay stopped by to collect his debt. "I thought I'd save you the trouble of seeking me out. I had a ship heading for Genoa that left shortly after yours. Mine returned earlier this week, so surely yours has as well."

Ambrose was certain the cur knew the *Mermaid Queen*, hadn't returned, but he remained congenial. "Now, Naughton, as you're aware, we agreed the debt would be paid off by the end of December. I suspect it just took a little longer for my captain to sell his cargo and buy goods. After all, it is his first time to Genoa."

But Ambrose was worried. He had the bulk of his money tied up in those shipments. If he dipped into clan funds, he'd probably have enough to pay his debt if it came to that, but doing so might not leave him with enough to keep Clan Ruthven going through the winter. He had left Dundee early this morning, wanting to put this worry behind him. After all, he did have until December and even if something had delayed the *Mermaid Queen*, there was still the ship bound to Venice, the *Merry Mistress*.

Then his carriage had been attacked on the road. Attacks happened from time to time, that's why noblemen traveled with guards. But when his guards were forced to fight, they made a pitiful showing. If the Highlanders hadn't arrived when they did, his men would have all been killed.

And Vida…

He took a swig of whisky. It was unbearable to think of what might have happened to her. By contrast to the Highlanders—hell, by contrast to the thieves—his men had been an embarrassment.

Then, as if all of that weren't enough, when he reached Cotharach he'd learned that there had been another raid on his land. Just one more in a series which his men had been unable to stop. Together with his guards' poor performance, he could no longer ignore how badly trained his men were in general.

He sighed, drained his glass, and headed towards his bedchamber, stopping to check on Vida as he went. To his surprise, she was still awake.

"Papa, you look worried."

"I'm just tired, pet."

She smiled the smile that never failed to melt his heart. "Papa, I know you're tired, but you're worried, too. What's the matter?"

Vida ran the household perfectly. She knew every detail of what happened at Cotharach. She also understood much of his shipping business. She was bright and good with numbers. But she didn't know about his debt to Lindsay, and he had no intention of sharing that with her. Still, he could tell her part of what was on his mind.

"Vida, my darling, what happened on the road tonight…I'm sorry, lass."

"It wasn't your fault. And everything ended well. Laird Carr and his men saw to that."

"But that's what I mean. Our men were nearly worthless."

Her brows drew together. "Aye, I must admit I expected better. But then I know nothing about your garrison."

"I thought you knew everything that went on around here," he teased.

She smiled, "Oh, I know all the boring details. How much they eat, for example. But I don't know anything really important like what skills they have…or lack."

He nodded. "Aye. It appears I don't either. And there was another raid while we were gone."

"I heard. Ten sheep and seven head of cattle."

"That's just one more sign my men don't know what they're doing."

"Honestly, Papa, I thought the same thing."

"I just don't know what to do about it."

"Those Highlanders made short work of the thieves."

"Aye, they did. But, of course, there were a lot of them."

"I know, but Sir Tomas faced one man alone. Like I told you in the carriage, he gave the thief two chances to surrender and when the man refused, well, the fight was over almost before it had started. It happened so fast. I'd never seen a man killed before. I've been thinking about it all evening."

"Oh, Vida, I'm so sorry."

"It's fine, Papa. It's not the dead man that drew my thoughts. I've been thinking about how skilled with a blade Sir Tomas is. And I also was wondering if…maybe…maybe you could talk to Laird Carr. Perhaps he'd allow you to hire Sir Tomas and a few of the others to stay here, even if only for a few months, in order to better train our men."

Ambrose thought about that. *Ask the Highlanders to stay?* He wanted to bring his men's skill levels up to a reasonable level. Based on what he'd seen and what Vida told him, these men might very well be able to do far better than that. And if his men could learn to fight even half as well…

"That could be the answer, Vida. If it becomes known that my men are a force to be reckoned with, the raids will stop and the clan will be safer in general."

"So, you'll ask Laird Carr? First thing tomorrow?"

"Aye, I will."

She took his hand. "Papa, first thing. If you delay, Carr and his men could be gone on their way back to the Highlands."

"I promise. First thing."

~ * ~

Vida said goodnight to her father and watched him leave. She loved him with everything in her, but she was not blind to his faults. He could lose his temper at the slightest provocation, but never in her presence. From an early age, she had learned how to use this to the advantage of the clan. If she could foresee that a situation might anger him, she made sure she was with him when confronting it. If she couldn't foresee it, she stepped in as soon as possible.

She had gone with him to Dundee for that very reason. She knew he worried about the risk he'd taken by sending not one, but two ships to Italian ports. If he received bad news when she wasn't with him…well, she didn't like to think about it.

And over the years, she believed he had mellowed. He generally didn't lose his temper over small things and didn't become quite so angry over bigger things. Of course, their clan members also made every attempt not to do the things that set him off. Still, peace reigned at Cotharach much more often than it once had.

She also knew that her father was an exceedingly proud man. He'd be unlikely to have ever thought of asking Laird Carr for help. And even if it had occurred to him, he'd probably refuse to consider it because it would mean admitting his failings and the clan's vulnerability to another leader. He only listened and accepted it because it had been her idea. That's why she had extracted the promise she did. She could imagine him going to bed, talking himself out of it and then claiming to have overslept to avoid the issue.

But, just in case, she intended to be downstairs at first light. If her father "overslept," she would take matters into her own hands. That might be less embarrassing for him anyway. She'd have to bind her ankle and use a walking stick, but she wouldn't let the opportunity pass.

She smiled to herself, wishing that Sir Tomas could be pressed into duty to carry her back downstairs in the morning. He was exceedingly handsome and although the way he'd dealt with her kidnapper had initially scared her, it didn't take long for her to recognize his honorable nature. She'd heard of men going berserk in the heat of battle, but he had been in complete control throughout the whole thing. At no time did he lose his temper. In fact, he had calmly offered the man his life—twice.

She sincerely hoped Laird Carr would consider their request and she prayed that if he did, Sir Tomas would be among the men he'd leave at Cotharach.

CHAPTER 3

Vida did awaken before dawn. Her ankle was not quite as tender as it had been the previous evening, but she took care to bind it firmly with strips of linen. Yesterday, Emma had found a walking stick in case she needed it in the night.

She slowly made her way down the stairs. When she entered the great hall, some servants were already moving about quietly, preparing for breakfast, while the men-at-arms, who normally bedded down in the hall, as well as most of their visitors, slept a bit longer. However, Sir Tomas was awake and standing near the hearth.

She walked toward him and he turned on hearing her approach.

Concern filled his eyes. "Lady Vida, ye must rest that ankle or risk injuring it further. My mother's a healer. She's always said tolerating a little inconvenience to allow a small injury to heal is far better than suffering the major inconvenience that results when ye don't."

"She's probably right, but I couldn't stay abed with visitors. Still, I can rest it sitting at the table. Will you join me?"

"Certainly, if it will get ye off yer feet." He took her elbow, escorted her to the laird's table, and helped her into a chair.

She asked, "Do you prefer wine or ale in the morning?"

"I don't often have the luxury of wine and I prefer ale in the morning, but ye needn't bother—"

"Don't be silly. I'm having some myself." She motioned to a serving girl. "Kenna, would ye bring us some ale and something with which to break our fast, please?"

"Aye, my lady."

"Truly, it isn't necessary," said Sir Tomas.

"You won't make me eat alone, will you?" Vida smiled at him.

"Nay, of course not."

"Good, because I'm famished."

Kenna returned quickly with two tankards of ale, bread, butter, cheese, ham, and small bowl of blackberry preserves.

"Help yourself, Sir Tomas."

"After ye, my lady. I believe it was ye who said ye're famished."

She laughed. "That I did." She buttered a slice of bread and, after laying a slice of ham on it, nibbled away.

He did likewise, but also cut a slice of cheese and ate.

"How long were ye at court, Sir Tomas?"

"Not long. Just a few days. We were delivering clan taxes to the crown."

"Ah, that explains why there were so many of you."

"Aye, it pays to take care when traveling with something of value."

"Yes, I'm sure it does." She remembered what he'd said to his horse about her being "precious cargo" and her cheeks warmed. "So, are you a Carr? I mean, were you raised in Clan Carr, or did you go there to train?"

"No, I trained elsewhere. With another Highland clan."

"You are clearly very skilled."

He frowned, looking a little uncomfortable. "I'm sorry ye had to witness that yesterday. He was kidnapping ye and I saw him strike ye as he pulled ye from the carriage."

He reached out a hand and brushed her hair from her face before tipping her chin up and nudging it to one side. With a feather light touch, he caressed her cheek. Then, he pulled his hand away and clenched his teeth. His eyes burned with anger. "He hurt ye. Only a feckless coward strikes a woman. That can't be allowed." He dropped his hand to the table. "I did give him the chance to save himself and stand trial."

She put a hand over his where it lay on the table. She had felt a connection to him when he touched her and she wasn't ready for it to end. "I know you did. That was very noble of you. It was a bit of a shock to see a man die like that, but you're right. I'm so very thankful you were there to save me."

"Think nothing of it."

"I can't. The entire event has opened my eyes."

"My lady, thieves abound. As long as ye're well protected, you will be fine."

"But that's the point, isn't it? We were not well protected. I thought we were, but my father's men didn't have the skills required. That worries me and not just for my own safety. Those men are among our best. Which means Cotharach, its village, and Clan Ruthven as a whole, are not well protected." The weight of that statement hit her with force. "I've let them down. I've worked all of these years to see to the needs of my clan and yet, I ignored its protection."

"*All of these years?* Ye're but a lass. My sister is eighteen and you can be no older than she is. Besides, isn't the management of the clan and ensuring the strength of its warriors yer father's responsibility?"

She frowned. When had the clan became her full responsibility? She started helping with things as soon as she had any skills. Father James had already taught her to read before her mother died. The elderly priest died a few years later, but Father Michael took his place and continued with her lessons. As soon as she could do sums, Manus showed her how the accounts were kept. "My father runs a trade and shipping company. He was often away, taking care of that business. I learned to help out here. I guess the clan began turning to me for some things when I was twelve or so. Gradually, they have become my responsibility."

"How could yer father put that on yer shoulders?"

"Oh, he didn't ask me to. I just…well…after my mother died, I just grew into it. I love my people and seeing to the clan's prosperity is an honor. But I realize I've failed them. And it's not just because of yesterday. We've lost too much livestock in raids over the last year. Clearly, we're perceived as weak, and I didn't know that until yesterday. What's more, I don't know what to do. I've always left the training of the men to their leaders."

~ * ~

Tomas could barely believe his ears. Ruthven wasn't married when Katherine left with him as a child. If Ambrose had been married the next day, there could still be no more than a few months between Vida and Beitris. Not only did Vida seem to run the clan, she blamed herself for the poor skills of their warriors. She was so like his mother. Not in looks, although there was a family resemblance. Nay, she was like Katherine in the deep commitment she felt to her clan. The same clan Katherine had once loved, cared for, and considered her responsibility.

"Lass, the state of the clan's garrison isn't yer fault. The training of men *is* up to their leaders. But yer father is ultimately their leader."

"Still…"

"Nay. Even if ye're responsible for every other aspect of clan life, ye aren't responsible for that. Yer unc…I mean yer da is the one to blame. If he wasn't capable himself, he needed to ensure the clan had skilled men to instruct them. I've been trained by some of the best warriors in the Highlands." He had nearly referred to Ambrose Ruthven as her uncle. It was hard to imagine that he fathered and raised the gentle, beautiful lass before him who felt such concern for her clan.

She smiled at him. "That's obvious."

Tomas glanced away, not wishing her to see how pleased he was by her compliment. It was only then that he noticed the other men were stirring. Vida must have noticed them too because she called for servants to set up trestle tables and bring food and ale.

He stood. "Pardon me, my lady, I've taken enough of yer time. I should gather my things. We'll be leaving soon."

"Of course, Sir Tomas, but 'tis I who must thank you for breaking your fast with me."

Did he imagine the disappointment he saw in her eyes? He bowed. "Ye're very welcome, my lady."

As Tomas walked away, he didn't know what to think. The Ambrose Ruthven who had entertained them last evening had been jovial and generous. Not remotely like the man Tomas remembered. Of course, Ambrose owed them a great deal. He saw more of the man he remembered in the discussion with Vida. Not the abusive tyrant, but the man who gave little thought to the clan and had left it in Katherine's hands.

It angered Tomas to think Vida blamed herself for their unskilled men-at-arms. Ruthven had paid no more attention to his garrison nineteen years ago than he did now. This problem had been brewing since before she was born. *Hell*, it had probably been brewing since Katherine's father died.

He knelt to roll up his blanket, then he attached the sword to his belt. Laird Carr had decided they would leave as soon as the sun was up. They'd make camp tonight. They should be able to reach Castle Carr easily the next day where they'd bid farewell to the Carrs. Brathanead, the MacLennan keep, was two days beyond that, and Duncurra wasn't a full day's ride from there. Under other circumstances, he might be tempted to stay a few days at Brathanead, but now he just wanted to go home and away from old unpleasant memories.

No sooner had the idea of putting bad memories behind him crossed his mind than his most unpleasant memory walked into the great hall.

"Good morning, Laird Carr. I trust you and your men slept well. Please join me at my table to break your fast."

"Thank ye, Laird Ruthven. We won't trouble ye much longer, though. We need to be on the road soon."

"But you must eat first. Come, join me." Ambrose walked toward the table, only just then noticing Vida. "Vida, my sweet, you shouldn't be up. You need to rest your ankle." He kissed her when he reached the table.

"I'm fine, Papa. It is wrapped snuggly and I used a walking stick. Which is exactly what I told Sir Tomas when he also chastised me. He was kind enough to help me to the table when I first came down. I won't overdo today. I promise."

Ambrose smiled broadly. "Sir Tomas helped you again. That's quite a fine man you have there, Laird Carr. Quite a fine man indeed."

Laird Carr gave a small nod. "As I said yesterday, I am glad we were able to be of some service."

"Oh, you were, you were. In fact, I wanted to talk to you about that."

"Certainly," said Laird Carr as he joined Ruthven at the table.

"Yesterday's events have forced me to face a rather unpleasant fact. The men in my garrison don't have the skills they should. Not only was their ability to protect me and my daughter inadequate, I have been suffering more and more raids, which they are unable to stop."

"I'm sorry for yer trouble, Laird Ruthven."

"Thank you, Laird. But in realizing my failings, I must do something about it and I was hoping I could enlist your aid in that."

Laird Carr's brows drew together and he slowly shook his head. "I'm not certain I can be of much assistance. I must return to my clan."

"I understand that, Laird, but I thought perhaps you could leave a few of your guardsmen here for a while—maybe six months? They could act as trainers and work with my men on improving their skills."

Tomas could scarcely believe his ears. Ambrose Ruthven had nerve asking such a thing.

"I don't know, Laird Ruthven. My men are needed at home."

"But you have so many here with you. Surely, you could spare a few. Perhaps just three? I will make it worth your while—and theirs. I'll pay you handsomely and enter into an alliance with you. I will never give you cause to regret improving the safety of my clan. I'll never turn those skills against ye."

Laird Carr's frown deepened and he tapped his fingers on the table.

By all that was holy, he wasn't considering this outrageous proposal.

Finally, Laird Carr said. "I'm sorry, Laird, I really don't think we can do this."

Vida had remained silent during this entire exchange, but at this, she made an appeal. "Please, Laird Carr, I know what we are asking is extraordinary. I know, too, we've brought this on ourselves by being less than diligent. But we don't ask this for ourselves. Rather, it is on behalf of our people who are in danger and may perish without your assistance."

Laird Carr sighed. "My lady, I appreciate yer candor and I do understand yer desire to protect yer people. Let me consider this for a bit and confer with my men, privately. They have families to consider as well."

Ruthven nodded. "Of course, of course. I understand. Perhaps you'd like to use our chapel. You'll have privacy there."

"Thank ye, Laird. I'll bring ye my final answer shortly." He rose from the table. "Guardsmen, with me." His son and Heck, the other of his guardsmen, rose and followed. Quinn, Kieran, Drew, Rowan, and Ethan went also. This was definitely a discussion Tomas didn't want to have, but he too joined them.

Once they gained the privacy of the chapel, Laird Carr addressed them. "Men, I can honestly say I've never found myself in this kind of a predicament before. Ruthven has a history of being a cruel, self-absorbed tyrant. Lady Vida is absolutely correct. They brought this on themselves, or at least, her father did. He is, without a doubt, unfit to lead. But she's also right in that it's their people who will suffer most if the situation is not rectified. Sadly, although she didn't say it, she may be most likely to bear the brunt of her father's failure. A clan with an eye to expansion could easily lay siege and be victorious. In fact, it might be just such a clan who is perpetrating the raids—testing to see how far they can go before simply launching an all-out attack. It isn't likely anyone will do such a thing coming into winter. They'll let the clan suffer increasing small losses and then attack in the spring. When that happens, she will be at their mercy."

He frowned and glanced away. Laird Carr had four daughters and numerous granddaughters. His concern for Lady Vida's safety was evident. "So, we are faced with a painful choice. I obviously cannot stay. And we are expecting Edward's betrothed and her family in November, so he cannot either. Rowan, Tomas, what do ye think Laird MacIan would wish to do?"

Rowan shook his head. "I can't say for sure. He has no love for Ambrose Ruthven, that's a fact. But it's not likely he'd be blind to Lady Vida's plight. He might offer to take her to safety until Ruthven deals with this mess himself."

Tomas agreed. "Aye, he'd be willing to do that. Lady Vida is my mother's cousin."

"For that matter, I could make the same offer," said Laird Carr.

"But I think we all know," said Quinn, "Ruthven's problems will not be easily fixed even if he had the ability to do it himself—which he doesn't. Besides, Lady Vida seems devoted to her clan. I doubt she'd willingly leave them as things are."

"Aye, I can't argue that either," said Laird Carr. "That was a very impassioned statement she made, and frankly, the only reason I'm entertaining her father's request."

"For what it's worth," said Quinn, "Laird MacLennan wouldn't require it, but if any of his men chose to remain for a short time, he'd allow it. Although, he wouldn't want anyone staying alone. And as sympathetic as I am, I have a family who needs me and I cannot stay."

Laird Carr nodded. "I agree, I'm unwilling to leave only a single warrior. If one of ye decide to remain here, I'd prefer at least three of ye do so. Heck's wife is expecting in December, and Rowan has a family too. Both of them need to return to their homes."

Quinn laughed. "Aye, that bold Fraser lass Rowan married would string him up by his cods if he doesn't come walking through their door by the end of the week."

Rowan grinned but didn't disagree.

"That leaves the MacBains and Ethan. And, of course, ye, Tomas, but I certainly would understand it if ye didn't wish to stay here."

"I would be willing to. Lady Katherine would want it," said Kieran, who had trained at Duncurra and knew her well. "My baby sister is to be married in November and I'd hate to miss that."

"Ye're right, about Lady Katherine. This was her clan," said Ethan. "But ye shouldn't miss yer sister's wedding. I'll stay if these other two can be talked into it."

Drew nudged Tomas in the ribs. "What do ye say, Tomas? It'll be fun. Like when we were in training, except we'll be the ones in charge now."

Tomas considered everything. As much as he wanted to turn his back and say no, what they'd said about his mother was absolutely true. She loved this clan every bit as much as she loved the MacIans. Hadn't she shown her love for him, the very least of her clansmen, by wrapping her body around his and taking the lashes meant for him? What's more, this was his clan too. The fact that Ambrose was at the head of it was no one's fault but the late King David's. Finally, Tomas said, "I'll stay. But only for a short time. We'll head for home when the weather breaks in February…if not sooner. By then, if the Ruthven men are not vastly improved, we'll offer to escort Lady Vida to her cousin for her safety."

Laird Carr nodded. "Agreed. And for what it's worth, I know this decision was hard, but I think ye've made the right one."

"I hope so, sir," said Tomas.

"Just remember, the three of ye are here on yer own terms. If it simply isn't working, if the men cannot be trained, or if the situation changes and siege is imminent, don't remain a day longer. Ye don't owe them anything, certainly not yer lives. Offer a safe home to Lady Vida and leave. If ye push, ye're only a hard day's ride from Castle Carr—a day and a half at the most."

The three young men agreed.

"Also, whether ye tell Laird Ruthven who ye really are, is up to ye. I suspect it is better to remain silent, at least for the moment. I'll see that yer lairds receive the gold he pays me for yer service. The agreement never to bear arms against my clan is probably only of real value to me, as my

Ceci Giltenan

holding is nearest to Ruthven. He's not likely to march into the Highlands after the MacIans or the MacLennans and he'd have to go through my territory to get there anyway."

When they returned to the great hall, a hush fell.

Laird Carr addressed their host. "Laird Ruthven, after consulting with my guardsmen, I have decided to leave three men with ye: Ethan MacLeod, Drew MacBain, and Tomas MacHenry.

Had Tomas imagined Lady Vida's small smile when Laird Carr said he'd be one of the men staying?

CHAPTER 4

Tomas, Drew, and Ethan began working with Ruthven's men that morning after Laird Carr left with the rest. Ruthven introduced them to the captain of his guard, Gregor Hay, before returning to the keep.

Tomas had faint memories of Gregor. He had been Laird Ruthven's squire for years and had become a member of his guard before Tomas and Katherine left. Mainly, Tomas remembered that his grandfather had liked Gregor. His grandfather judged men by a simple rule, "Don't trust a man who doesn't treat his beasts well. It's a sure sign something rotten lurks beneath." Tomas's adoptive father had a similar belief, "A good man respects his mount and treats it with the care he'd give his own sword arm, for they are extensions of each other." Tomas had memories of Gregor, in the stable, helping to take care of horses.

As soon as Ruthven had left them, Tomas said, "Perhaps we should just start by watching yer men train?"

"Sir, I think we should start with an apology. I am sorry, and ashamed that it was necessary for the laird to ask ye to do this."

Tomas shook his head. "First, just call me Tomas, not sir. I think that goes for all of us." He glanced at Drew and Ethan, who indicated their agreement. "And second, ye needn't apologize. The person responsible for ensuring that his garrison is adequately trained is the laird. Ye can only do what ye can do with what ye have. Our purpose here is not to lay blame, but rather to teach ye what we can."

Gregor offered him his hand. "Thank ye."

They spent the rest of the day watching the Ruthven men train. Afterward, they sat down with Gregor to discuss what they'd learned.

Tomas said, "It isn't that ye're men aren't skilled. I suspect they have had very skilled instruction, but from only a few men, so it has been limited. They go through the exact same exercises over and over. If an opponent approached them in that way, he'd be sliced down."

Ethan nodded. "Aye, but when there is any variation, they have to decide what to do and in those infinitesimal delays, an opponent with more skill can gain the upper hand."

"We can help round out their skills," said Drew. "Tomas and I are among the finest swordsmen in the Highlands, because of the way we were trained. And Ethan's not bad either," he teased.

"I've kicked yer arse on occasion," said Ethan with a grin.

"Well, I'd appreciate any help ye can give us," said Gregor.

"What's more concerning," said Tomas, "is the fact that ye've suffered as many raids as ye have. It tells me that whoever is doing this is growing more and more confident of their success and your inability to defend against them. We have to prove them wrong. As far as I can tell, you send out men to patrol your borders in a fairly predictable pattern."

"That's a bit like training with the same exercises," said Ethan. "Your enemies learn how to avoid you."

"So, we change our routine?" asked Gregor.

Tomas grinned slyly. "Nay, ye don't. Ye keep sending the two patrols of four men exactly as ye have been. But ye send others too, and those are the ones whose movements ye vary. If ye double yer number of patrols, and have four groups of men out every night, two of which use more covert tactics, you will stop the next raid."

Drew said, "We'll put eight men in each of the other two patrols. One of us will go with them the first few times as a training exercise."

"Why eight men?" asked Gregor.

Tomas answered, "It is unlikely that more than four men are doing the thieving. It would be easier to detect them if they were using men than that. Additionally, they aren't taking huge numbers of beasts, only what they can manage to move quickly. Eight men with average skills—and yer men do have average or better skills—can easily prevail against four. We don't want lives lost."

Ethan added. "The predictable patrols can continue to be just four men for a while because we're fairly sure your enemy is making every effort to avoid them."

Tomas nodded. "As soon as we thwart one raid, we'll increase the number of men on the other patrols and stop the established pattern altogether. One failed attempt will be enough to tell them ye've changed yer tactics and hopefully tell us who's behind it. They'll be more cautious then next time."

"But if I send twenty-four men out every night, and others are busy guarding the keep, how will we accomplish any training?" asked Gregor.

"It's easier than ye might think," answered Tomas. "Ye have two men at the gate and another six on the wall at all times and they are on duty for four hours at a time. Ye have a total of about one hundred men?"

"Aye, a hundred and three to be precise."

Tomas said, "Well, divide them into four groups of at least twenty-four men and they will cycle posts every three days. One group will ride patrols. Two groups will split their time between guarding the keep and training. Each man will work four hours at a guard post and will train for four hours either in the morning or the afternoon. The remaining group will train both morning and afternoon for three days. We won't train on Sundays."

"That means in twelve weeks, each man will train for eighteen full days and thirty-six half days. Each man will guard the keep for four hours on forty-two days including six Sundays, they'll serve patrol on twenty-one days including three Sundays, and they'll have three Sundays completely off," said Drew.

Tomas said, "It's a fairly intense schedule, but we will only be here until February. If after one twelve-week cycle, everything is going extremely well, ye can make changes. Reduce the number of men on patrol to eighteen, give the men who serve watch between midnight and prime the day off from training. Ye can decide based on the situation then."

Gregor nodded. "Aye, we'll start tomorrow."

"We'll start tonight," said Tomas. "Ethan will take sixteen men out tonight to begin training them to patrol. He has stellar tracking skills. Drew will take them then next night, and I'll take the next. We'll rotate like that until we're comfortable that everyone is well enough trained at patrolling to leave them on their own."

Gregor smiled. "All right. I want to go, so I'll select seven more."

Ethan smiled. "Good. We'll leave immediately after supper and return after daybreak."

~ * ~

After Laird Carr had left with his men, Vida had given in to Emma's nagging and returned to her chamber to stay off of her injured ankle. She soaked it from time to time in cool water. The swelling had gone down considerably by evening, however, and she refused to stay locked away in her chamber. She wanted to be at the table and hear the discussions of how the day of training had gone with the Carr warriors.

When the Carrs entered the hall with Gregor and some of the other men, Vida was glad that her father called for them to join him at his table. If he hadn't, Vida would have, but it was better that the invitation came from him. She simply had to listen to the conversations to learn all she needed to.

"So," asked her father, "how did things go today? Please tell me my men aren't hopeless."

Sir Tomas laughed. "They aren't hopeless. Far from it. They have just been exposed to less variety. The skills they have are very good. They have had excellent instruction, but men can only teach what they themselves have learned. Our skills aren't necessarily better, just different because we've had different experiences. So, it's really just a matter of broadening their skills by exposing them to diverse techniques."

Vida was amazed. With a few words, Tomas had managed to give both her father and Gregor a bit of their pride back.

Tomas and Drew talked about honing instincts and shortening reaction times and her father was rapt. At one point he asked, "I wish I were younger. I'd like to learn these things as well."

"Laird Ruthven," said Drew, "Laird Carr has more than three score years to his credit and he still trains some every day."

"Does he? But he has such a capable guard. Surely he no longer needs to defend himself."

A frown flitted briefly across Sir Tomas's face. "Laird Carr prefers not to let other men fight for him. As long as he can lift a sword, he'll fight beside them. The only way he can do that is to keep his skills as sharp as possible."

"Then you think I could train with the men?"

Drew nodded. "If ye wish."

Ruthven turned to address Tomas directly. "Will you work with me, Sir Tomas?"

Vida couldn't quite read the expression on Tomas's face. For a fleeting moment, it seemed as if he were horrified, but it must simply have been shock or surprise. In fairness,

Vida herself was surprised. For years her father hadn't done more than occasionally spar briefly with Gregor.

"Aye…uh…if that's what ye wish," answered Tomas.

"I don't want to take away from the time ye spend with my men, but aye, I'd like that."

"Well, then…uh…perhaps ye'd like to join us tomorrow after the midday meal?"

"That would be perfect." Her father smiled, appearing truly happy. "I'm looking forward to it."

Sir Tomas and Sir Drew also explained the problem they had identified with the way the Ruthven men patrolled the holding. Her father asked questions, appearing truly interested. "Can I ride patrol with you one night?"

Both of the Carr men frowned.

"Sir, I appreciate yer desire to learn," said Sir Tomas, "But I fear ye'd be putting yerself in harm's way. It would be better to wait until I'm certain yer men can protect ye well. The last think we'd want would be for ye to be taken hostage."

"Aye, then it's probably best to wait a while on that."

The talk of the day's training went on throughout the evening meal, Sir Gregor and a few of the other Ruthven knights joining in to praise the Carrs. When supper was over, her father rose from the table. "I'm going to retire for the evening. Please enjoy yourselves. Vida, shall I help you up to bed?"

"No, thank you, Papa. I'll come up in a bit."

"Very well. I'm certain Sir Tomas will help you up the stairs if you need it."

She could barely contain a chuckle. If it was possible, her father gave every appearance of being *smitten* by Sir Tomas. "Aye, Papa, I'm sure he would, but I think I'll be fine."

The men dispersed from the tables and the servants cleaned up the remnants of the meal and took down the trestles. To her disappointment, Sir Tomas too rose to go with the men. She wanted to spend a little more time in his company, but to do that she had to think of a way to keep him from leaving. "Uh…Sir Tomas…I…uh…do you play chess?"

"Do I…I'm sorry, did ye ask if I play chess?"

She smiled at him in the way she did if she needed her papa to do something. "Aye, I did. Do you? Play chess, that is?"

"Aye, of course."

"Would you care to play with me?"

A salacious grin spread across his face and Vida felt a hot blush rise in her cheeks.

"I…I…I mean, chess. Would you care to play *a game of chess* with me?"

"Aye. I'd be happy to play *a game of chess* with ye."

"Emma," she called. "Would you mind bringing me my chessboard and have Nuala bring us wine?"

"Certainly, my lady."

Sir Tomas sat back down. Vida wasn't sure why she'd done that. She'd never desired to spend time in any man's company. But then, Sir Tomas MacHenry wasn't just any man. He was the very attractive young man who had saved her from a kidnapper. Plus, he appeared to have won her father's affection, which was beyond amusing.

"Do you make a habit of playing chess in the evening?" he asked.

"I used to. I played with Papa nearly every evening. But over the last few years, he has grown less fond of the game. I can usually coax Father Michael into a game if he's free."

"And no one else will play with ye?"

"Sometimes, if we have guests such as yourselves, I can find someone willing to play, but otherwise, nay."

Vida noticed Moyna, the elderly woman in charge of the kitchens and not the young maid Nuala, hurrying towards her from the back of the hall bearing a tray with a ewer of wine and two goblets.

"Moyna, you didn't have to bring that yourself."

"'Tis no trouble, my lady. I did want to be certain you didn't want to make any changes to tomorrow's meals."

Vida smiled. She suspected the truth was that the older woman just wanted to get a look at their guests. "Nay, what you've planned is fine."

"Very well, my lady." Moyna bobbed a curtsy.

"Moyna, this is Sir Tomas MacHenry, one of Laird Carr's men. Sir Tomas, this is Moyna. She's in charge of the kitchens here."

Sir Tomas stood, turned towards Moyna, and gave a small bow. "It's very nice to meet you, Moyna."

Moyna's eyes widened, then her brows drew together in confusion. "Sir Tomas? Sir Tomas *MacHenry*, you say?

"Aye, Moyna, this is Sir Tomas MacHenry. Surely ye've heard that three of Laird Carr's men are staying at Cotharach to help better train our men-at-arms."

Moyna's gaze seemed fixed on Sir Tomas's face as if searching for something. "Aye, my lady," she answered distractedly. "I'm pleased to meet you, *Sir Tomas*. Very pleased, indeed. If you need anything, anything at all, just ask. 'Tis a very good thing you do."

"Thank ye, Moyna," said Tomas, bowed again. He didn't seem to find her behavior strange.

"Excuse me, please. I'll just go back to the kitchen." Moyna bobbed another curtsy and hurried out of the hall.

Vida smiled and poured a goblet of wine for Sir Tomas as he sat back down. "Pardon her unusual behavior. I suspect she's been curious about our visitors all day and could wait no longer."

"Ye've nothing to apologize for. She seems very kind."

Emma finally arrived with the chess set. Vida set it up and, taking a pawn in each hand, put her hands behind her back then presented him with her closed fists. "Which hand do you wish, Sir Tomas."

"Please, just call me Tomas."

"Tomas, then. But in that case, you must just call me Vida."

He smiled. "Very well. I'll take the left hand, Vida." She turned over her palm to reveal the black pawn.

~ * ~

Tomas took the pawn from her hand. "White goes first, make your move."

Initially he was distracted, thinking of Moyna. She appeared to recognize him. That she didn't acknowledge it was good. He would have to try and find a way to talk with her. But after the first few less than well thought out moves, Tomas realized he had to focus while playing chess with Vida. He also thought he might have an inkling why no one, especially her father, would play with her—they didn't like to lose. She was exceedingly good and he lost the first game in minutes.

"Ah, Vida, I made the classic mistake of underestimating my foe. Will ye allow me to redeem myself?"

She gave him a heart-stopping smile. "Of course. I'd love to play another game."

This time he was prepared and paid closer attention.

Perhaps trying to distract him, she asked lots of questions about the Highlands, his home, and Clan Carr. He did his best to answer without telling too many lies.

"Tomas, tell me, is it usual for men to name their horses?"

"That's an odd question, why do you ask?"

"I just heard once that seasoned warriors don't name their horses, but you called your horse Duff."

"I don't know if it's usual everywhere, but the warriors I know name their horses. A horse is not a piece of equipment. It is a living creation of God, and in battle, an extension of oneself. I've heard some men name their swords. It seems much more reasonable to me for them to name a beast they depend on."

"Oh, I agree. I can't imagine not having a name for my horse."

"Do you have a horse?" asked Tomas.

Her face lit up. "Yes. A black mare. I named her Mab, after the fairy queen."

"Really?" Tomas was shocked. "I named my first pony Mab."

"You're teasing me."

"Nay, I'm serious. An older girl in the clan had told me fairy stories and Mab was always in them."

"What an odd coincidence. I've never heard of another horse named Mab. Even when I named her, some of my more superstitious clansmen warned me that I might be tempting the fairies to work some mischief."

Tomas laughed, "I never thought about that. I just really liked the name when I was a wee lad." His grin broadened as another memory came to him.

"What amuses you so?"

"I was just remembering that I liked the name so much, I wanted my parents to name my baby sister Mab."

She laughed and Tomas delighted in the sound. It enveloped him in a sweet warmth.

"How many brothers and sisters do you have?"

Damn. Tomas had inadvertently revealed more than he wished anyone at Cotharach to know. He'd have to tread carefully. "I have two brothers and a sister."

"Older or younger?"

"All younger."

"Are any of them married? Do you have nieces and nephews who are pining for Uncle Tomas? For that matter, are you married?"

"Nay, I'm not married and neither are any of them. They're all much younger. My youngest brother is twelve. My sister's the oldest of them and she's but eighteen."

"My age. Exactly how much older are you?"

He chuckled. He had answered this battery of questions before. Young women at court, anxious to find husbands were no less obvious. "I'm twenty-six, my lady."

"Eight years between you and your next oldest sibling. My goodness."

"I was adopted."

"Oh, I see."

"And your father? Is he one of Laird Carr's guardsmen?"

"Nay." Tomas said no more. A discussion about his parents was best avoided and the easiest way to do that was to change the subject. "Who taught ye to play chess?"

She smiled sadly. "My mother started to teach me when I was a very little girl. I learned how the pieces moved and captured other pieces. Before she died, we played some. But mostly I loved just playing with the pieces like they were dolls. I imagined them to be two royal families, with lots of children." Vida smiled and blushed. "Mama would play that with me too sometimes. I thought it would be fun to live in a big family."

"Do ye not have cousins?" Tomas knew full well she did—but she might not know that.

"I have cousins in my mother's family. We visited them some when she was alive, but not since then."

"And yer father?"

"He had an older brother who died."

"What about his children?"

"My uncle didn't have any children. At least, I don't think he did. None that lived anyway. If he'd had children, my papa wouldn't have become laird."

Tomas scowled. *By all the angels, Ruthven never told her about Katherine.*

"Is something wrong?"

He shook his head, forcing a smile. "Nay, lass, I'm just trying to figure out how to get out of the corner ye've boxed me into. Ye didn't learn to play chess like this by pretending the pieces were dolls. Did yer da continue yer lessons?"

"Nay. Well, I suppose in a way he did. He wanted me to learn how to read and write and do sums. So, he had our priest teach me." A warm smile spread across her face. "Father James, was wonderful. He taught me so much more than just those basic skills, including chess. He died when I was ten and it was nearly as painful as when mama died." She sighed. "But he was elderly and in his last year he'd become very frail. He said he was ready for the angels to lead him into paradise."

Tomas remembered Father James. He was exceedingly kind and Lady Katherine had adored him. Tomas had known he must have surely passed away by now, but his heart ached a little anyway. Almost without thinking, he made the sign of the cross and said a silent prayer for his soul.

Vida had a slightly bemused look on her face. "That was kind of you."

"I'm sorry, what?"

"Saying a prayer for the soul of a stranger. It was kind."

A stranger. Right. Tomas had to be more careful. "I…uh…I have known priests who were dear to me. And I suppose it never hurts to pray for the soul of a priest."

"Nay, I don't suppose it does. But it was kind of you anyway."

They played in silence for a few minutes. He realized she was only three moves from checkmate and he had no way of preventing it. Then, to his surprise, she made a move that killed her chance at checkmate and created an opening for him to win. He'd seen enough of her skill so far to know she'd thrown the game intentionally.

He frowned at her, irritated. "Don't do that."

"What?" Her tone was innocent, but her eyes told a different story.

"Put that piece back and make the move ye'd intended to make."

"I…I…don't know what you mean."

His eyes narrowed, as his irritation shifted slowly to anger. "Don't pretend ye don't know what ye just did. Make the correct move. *Now*."

Her eyes grew suspiciously bright and she blinked as if trying to hold back tears. She looked down, quickly and replayed the move.

He hadn't intended to make her cry. But her pretending to lose was not only insulting to him, it demeaned her. One of her hands rested on the table and he covered it with his. "Lass, ye're an extremely skilled chess player. Truly one of the best I've ever encountered. Don't belittle that by intentionally losing."

"I'm sorry. It's just…I…most people…"

He suspected he knew what she was trying to say. He reached out, putting a finger under her chin, tilting her head up so he could look into her eyes. "I don't need to win to enjoy the game. I'm sorry you've played with people who do."

She swallowed hard and nodded.

The game ended quickly, but she didn't meet his eyes when she said checkmate.

He knocked over his king, conceding the win. "Vida, ye're a worthy opponent. Especially for one whose tutelage ended when ye were ten."

Her smile returned. "My *tutelage* didn't end when I was ten. Father James was a smart man and a reasonably good chess player, but Father Michael is a master of the game and, frankly, ruthless."

"So, he's the only one who can best ye?"

She laughed outright, the warmth of it filling him again. "Aye, occasionally, but he doesn't best me very often. You, however, are every bit as skilled."

"Thank ye, my lady."

"You agreed to call me Vida."

"Well then, thank you, *Vida*. I look forward to our next match."

Her eyes widened in surprise. "Really? You'll play with me again?"

He grinned.

She blushed. "Stop it. You know what I mean. You'll play *chess* with me again?"

"Of course, I will. It never pays to sit back and think one knows everything. The only way I will continue to improve my chess game is to play with people who can best me."

She canted her head. "I guess it's a bit like what ye told Papa at supper, about our men. They're skilled, but only as skilled as the men who taught them, and the only way to improve is to be exposed to new methods."

"Exactly. I would be doing them a disservice if I didn't give my best when sparring. It is the only way they'll learn. Empty victory is meaningless. And I can promise ye this, if I do eventually win a game of chess with ye, the victory will be sweet."

She grinned, her eyes twinkling with mirth. "Don't count on it happening anytime soon."

Tomas laughed. "I wouldn't dream of it."

"Well then, Tomas, speaking of dreams, it's getting late. I should retire."

"Will ye allow me to help ye up the stairs?"

She stood and tested her ankle by bearing weight on it. Pain flashed briefly across her face, but she said, "I think I'll be fine."

"Vida, ye're going to have to stop hiding things. Ye're ankle hurts and ye'll do yerself no favors by bearing weight on it if ye don't have to. Now, I'm going to ask again, will ye allow me to help ye up the stairs?"

She blushed, but gave him a small smile and said, "Aye. Thank ye."

"There's a good lass." He scooped her into his arms and headed towards the stairs.

Emma, who had been waiting at a discreet distance, rose, followed them, and then opened the door to Vida's chamber so he could carry her in.

Tomas deposited her on the bed. "I'll leave ye in Emma's care now. Good night, Vida."

"Good night, Tomas. Thank you."

"Ye're very welcome. I look forward to our rematch tomorrow."

The look of delight on her face caused something to stir deep in his belly.

"Until tomorrow then," she said, her eyes shining.

Tomas returned to the hall, found his blanket roll, and went to lay down near Drew who was already snoring. Although tired himself, the events of the day whirled through Tomas's thoughts. He had scarcely believed his ears when Ambrose Ruthven specifically asked to train with him. Improving Ruthven's ability to fight with a sword was the absolute last thing Tomas wanted to do and yet he'd agreed to it.

Thinking on it now, he wasn't sure how he would suppress the desire to run Ruthven through in the process. He grinned as he allowed himself to imagine that. If it happened, it would simply look like an accident. God knows Ruthven's aptitude for fighting must be rusty at best. Then Tomas set those thoughts aside. He couldn't intentionally kill a man he'd agreed to train. It would be akin to inviting someone to come for a feast and then murdering them before it was over.

Of course, he could always just build on bad techniques rather than correcting them and teaching new ones. But even as the thought occurred to him, he knew he couldn't do that either. His pride wouldn't allow it. If he was going to do this, he'd have to do it right. *Damn it all anyway.*

Do it right. A slow smile spread across his face as he realized that was the answer. Ruthven didn't like to play chess with Vida because he didn't like to lose. Tomas figured he wouldn't want to look weak either, especially not in front of his men. Training was physically and mentally challenging, so all Tomas had to do was push him as hard as he would any other man. Tomas figured it would take no more than three sessions for Ruthven to back out. Problem solved.

But he still couldn't sleep. His thoughts drifted to Vida.

She was wholly unexpected.

He loved that she was smart, her devotion to her clan was admirable, and beautiful didn't begin to describe her. Her coloring was striking. Dark hair, deep green eyes, and ruby lips contrasted with fair skin that pinked beautifully when she blushed. Just thinking about her stirred his desire.

This was madness. As soon as he accomplished what they'd set out to, he wanted nothing more to do with Ambrose Ruthven, his clan, or his daughter. He only wanted to go home. He vowed to keep a little more distance between himself and Vida. He would not lose his heart to a woman he could never have.

CHAPTER 5

October 11, 1378
Duncurra, the central Highlands

Niall was overseeing his men as they trained on the heath beyond Duncurra's village. He smiled, watching as Turcuil, an absolute giant of a man and the commander of Niall's guard, yelled praise, criticism, and instructions as he paced along the rows of sparring men.

Eventually, he came to stand beside Niall. "I'm getting too old for this."

Niall snorted. Turcuil was two score and sixteen, only seven years older than Niall himself. "Ye're certainly not too old. Ye can still best every man on that field."

Turcuil growled. "Of course, I can. But that doesn't mean I still have patience to teach the young eejits."

Niall laughed. "Ye don't fool me. I know ye love seeing the results."

Turcuil chuckled. "Aye, seeing them turn into warriors is rewarding, but the process is painful sometimes."

They were still discussing the strengths and weaknesses of the young men in training when one of Niall's younger guardsmen jogged towards them from the keep. Niall frowned. "Con, is something wrong?"

"I'm not certain, Laird. A small party approaches. It appears to be Rowan returning from the royal court."

"I was expecting them to return about now. What concerns ye?"

"There are only four riders, Laird."

Niall frowned. "Who's missing?"

"They're still far enough away that I can't be absolutely certain, but it appears that Tomas and Ethan aren't with them."

Niall's frown deepened.

"Laird, perhaps they decided to stay for a few extra days at Brathanead," said Turcuil.

"It's possible. But it wouldn't be like Rowan to not leave a couple of men with them."

"Don't borrow trouble," cautioned Turcuil.

"Aye. I won't. They'll be here soon enough and we'll know then."

"Laird, Lady Katherine had asked several days ago to be notified as soon as the party was spotted returning. Shall I tell her?"

"Nay."

Turcuil arched an eyebrow. "She won't be pleased when she finds out."

"Maybe not, but the fact is, what she actually wanted was to be notified when *Tomas* was returning. And he's not returning."

"You don't know that for sure," said Turcuil.

"All the more reason not to worry her. Con, if it becomes clear that Tomas is actually with them, ye can tell Lady Katherine. Otherwise, wait until I know what's happened."

"Aye, Laird," said Con before he turned and jogged back towards the village.

At Turcuil's continued look of disapproval, Niall said, "Ye know she'll be beside herself with worry until Rowan gets here and it isn't necessary. All that worry won't change anything. It's far better to be able to give her the whole story once we have it, whatever it is."

Turcuil shrugged. "I believe ye, thousands wouldn't."

When Rowan did arrive a little over an hour later, he came directly to Niall on the training field. It was true, Tomas and Ethan weren't with him, but thankfully they were in no danger.

"Laird, no one was anxious to help Ambrose Ruthven, but when we considered everything, we decided Lady Katherine would not want to leave her clan in danger."

Niall agreed. "Ye're right. She wouldn't. But she is going to worry herself sick over Tomas being one of the men who stayed." He sighed. "I need to go tell her."

Rowan nodded. "It's probably not a good idea to risk her seeing me riding up to Duncurra with them, Laird. You can ride Blaze back and give him over to a stable hand. I'll go straight to my cottage."

"Thank ye, Rowan. I'm sure yer wife will be glad to see ye home all the sooner." Niall mounted the horse and was back to the keep in minutes. He entered and found his lovely wife in the midst of preparing the hall for the evening meal. They had been married for more than nineteen years and, if possible, he loved her more every day.

"Niall, ye're back a bit earlier than usual this evening." She crossed the hall, stood on her tiptoes, and gave him a quick kiss.

That simply wouldn't do. He cupped her face in his hands and gave her deeper kiss, breaking it only when he heard titters of laughter from their daughter, Beitris. "That's enough from ye, young lady," he said in mock seriousness. "Surely ye're neglecting some task by standing there gawking."

She laughed, turning back to the cloth she was spreading on a table. "All right. Go about yer business, Da, and I'll mind my own."

"Katherine, come with me to our chamber for a few minutes."

She laughed. "Niall, can't this wait until after supper?"

"Nay, my bonnie lass, it can't."

She shrugged. "Very well. Beitris, finish seeing to things here. I'll be back shortly."

"Aye, Mama," she said with a cheeky grin that was so like her mother's. It was time he found a husband for her, but Niall simply wasn't ready for that yet.

"Naill?" said Katherine, stirring him from his thoughts. "Are we going to our chamber or not?"

"Aye, we are sweetling." He took her hand in his.

When they reached their chamber, she was barely through the door before she asked, "What's happened?"

"Why do ye think something's happened?"

She put her hands on her hips and cocked her head.

He shrugged. "Ye're right. I need to tell ye something. Rowan returned today, but Tomas and Ethan did not come with him."

"Why not?" she asked, her voice thick with concern.

He explained what had happened and Tomas's decision to stay and help the Ruthvens.

She was quiet when he had finished, appearing to consider what he'd told her. Then finally said, "He's right. I would want to help them. They are my people. I feared my uncle would ruin the clan, but everything we'd heard over the years sounded as if things were going well enough. What do ye think?"

"I'm proud of him. But I'm worried. Apparently, Hugh is most concerned by the blatant raids that have been occurring. He thinks, and I agree, that a neighboring clan is testing Ambrose. If they realize how weakened he really is, they'll lay siege."

"Oh dear God, Niall. Nay."

"There's no need to worry yet. Winter can only weaken an already struggling clan. If someone does have their eyes on Cotharach, they'll wait until spring to lay siege. Carr warned the three of them to leave as soon as the weather breaks in February."

"But ye know they won't. Not if they really think the clan is in danger."

"Aye. I'm afraid ye're right and Hugh suspects as much too."

"What are we going to do?"

"If we've heard nothing about how things are going by December, I'll send men to help."

She raised an eyebrow. "Won't it be odd for MacIan men to show up?"

Niall chuckled. "Aye, I suppose it would be. But they won't be MacIan men. Hugh has offered his assistance. He'll add a few of his own to the party and they'll ride under the Carr banner. I suspect a few MacLennans will go with them, given that Drew MacBain is there too."

"And there's nothing we can do until then?"

Niall pulled her into his arms and held her close. "Katherine, we raised him well. The fact that he elected to stay and do this in spite of Ambrose is testament to that. Tomas is a good man and a strong warrior. There's none better. Until something changes, let's rely on him.

CHAPTER 6

October 13, 1378
Ruthven territory

This was the third night Tomas had ridden patrol with Ruthven men. The first two nights he'd gone out with them had been dark and misty. Not the ideal conditions for someone unfamiliar with the terrain to be out raiding. So, it served as an excellent opportunity to instruct, without worrying about actually running in to reivers. And the Ruthvens were catching on quickly to the tactics Ethan, Drew, and now Tomas were teaching them.

Tomas had summed it up. "Basically, ye have to think and behave like thieves and raiders to catch them. Ye know yer land better than anyone. If ye were raiding it, how would ye do it? Where would ye enter the territory? Which farms are at the greatest risk? Once ye're aware of the weaknesses, then it's just a matter of moving quietly and staying hidden. Don't let the thieves know they aren't alone, until the last possible moment."

The weather this night was completely different. The sky was clear and the moon was a waning gibbous, high and bright in the wee hours of the morning. "Tonight, I want ye to put to use everything ye've learned. If I were going to help myself to another man's livestock, I'd pick a night like tonight to do it."

So, it didn't come as a surprise when Tomas found signs of recent riders having entered Ruthven territory near their eastern border. The men with him spread out and silently followed the path the trespassers left. Before long, they had the thieves surrounded and Tomas signaled the attack.

Initially, the thieves fought. Tomas had engaged the man who seemed to be their leader, based on the fact that he had been the one calling orders to others. His skills with a blade were good, but no match for Tomas, who toyed with him briefly before offering him his life and the lives of his men if he surrendered. The man glanced around, as if he were trying to determine if there was any chance they could escape. Evidently realizing there was none, he capitulated.

Once the men were disarmed. Tomas had them bound.

"Ye promised us our lives," said the leader.

"Aye, I did. And sure, aren't ye all still breathing as we speak?"

"For the moment, but what do ye intend to do with us? We'll hang if ye turn us over to the sheriff."

"I suppose ye might, but that wasn't my plan."

"Then what is your plan?"

"Now, ye see, I figure ye aren't just wandering thieves or a band of banished clansmen."

"How would you know that?"

"Ye were riding reasonably good horseflesh." Tomas picked up one of their swords and held it up. "And this isn't the sword of a poor man. But, most telling, ye knew how to use it well. Remarkably well. So, the way I see it, ye can tell me who yer laird is and Laird Ruthven will send him a polite letter offering to return ye hale and hearty...for a wee ransom."

"Ye're wrong. We're poor men just trying to feed our families."

Tomas nodded. "Ah, well then. 'Tis off to the Lord Sheriff with the lot of ye." Tomas turned to the Ruthven men, who seemed amused. "What do ye say lads? I reckon we can throw these miscreants over the backs of their horses and have them in Perth by morning."

"Aye. Easily," answered one of the Ruthvens.

Tomas shrugged. "Then let's get them on their mounts and we'll be on our way."

Two men grabbed one of the thieves and hoisted him over the saddle of one horse. They went for the leader next.

"No. Wait. Stop. Let me down and I'll tell ye who we are."

The men holding him looked to Tomas for direction. Tomas inclined his head slightly and the Ruthvens stood the thief on the ground.

"I'm waiting," said Tomas.

"We're Gows."

"And why has Laird Gow been raiding Ruthven land over the past few months?"

"He hasn't been. This is our first raid."

Tomas snorted. "Lads, if he's going to lie to us, just put him back on the horse."

The men made to lift him again.

"Stop. Let me go."

When Tomas didn't interfere, the man yelled. "Fine, it's not our first raid. Now put me down."

Tomas motioned for his men to do so. "So, I'll ask again. Why has Laird Gow been raiding Ruthven land over the past few months?"

"Because he could. He heard Ruthven was a soft target. But I swear to ye, on my life, this is only the third raid our Laird ordered."

Tomas knew there had been at least eight raids in the last six months. But he also believed the Gow clansman was telling the truth. Just as Laird Carr suspected, word regarding the Ruthvens was circulating. Now Tomas needed men to start spreading a different story. He made great show of inspecting the thieves' horses. They were indeed fine mounts. The blades and dirks they carried were high quality too.

Tomas addressed the leader again. "I appreciate the honesty. Thank ye. So, now all that's left to do is ransom ye. But truthfully, that's a bit of nuisance, wouldn't ye agree?

Hauling ye back to Cotharach. Locking ye in the dungeon. Sending messages back and forth, negotiating ransoms. It could take months. And also, the timing's a bit unfortunate for prisoners. Ye see, as winter comes on, the rats in the dungeon get a bit more aggressive. They're unpleasant bedmates to say the least."

The leader blanched.

"On the other hand, those are fine horses and yer weapons are valuable too." Tomas looked at them thoughtfully for a moment. "By the look of ye, I'd say it isn't likely ye're members of the laird's family, so ye won't bring a huge ransom anyway." Tomas shrugged. "To save us all a lot of bother, how about we accept yer arms and yer mounts in lieu of a ransom. Do ye agree?"

The man looked extremely relieved. "Aye. That's fair enough."

"Perfect. Now we'll help ye find yer way safely off our land. Mind ye, if I ever see any of ye in Ruthven territory again, I'll give ye no quarter. Is that clear?"

"Aye," said the leader.

"In fact, ye can tell yer laird, if I ever catch *any* other Gow on Ruthven land, uninvited, there won't be anything left to ransom. If ye give a whit about yer clansmen, ye'll make certain he understands that. Ye ken?"

"Aye. I do."

Tomas ordered their feet unbound but left their wrists tied behind their backs until they reached the Ruthven border, where they were released.

The leader walked a few paces, then turned and asked, "What in hell is a Highlander doing patrolling Ruthven land?"

Tomas laughed. "I'm on a wee holiday. This is what we do for fun."

The Ruthven men laughed and if Tomas wasn't much mistaken, a hint of a smile flirted on the Gow clansman's lips before he turned and walked away.

Tomas and his men stayed near the border until nearly sunup just to make sure the Gows didn't return. Clearly they weren't stupid for there was no further sign of them. When dawn broke, the Ruthven patrol headed back to Cotharach, with four fine horses, tack, and a small collection of weapons.

Tomas took care of Duff, and made a closer inspection of the Gows' horses before entering the keep. When he stepped through the doors of the great hall, a cheer went up. Clearly, news of the night's exploits preceded him. Both Drew and Ethan greeted him with hearty slaps on the back.

"On a wee holiday are ye?" asked Drew, laughing.

Tomas shrugged. "It seemed a reasonable answer, all things considered."

"Tomas, my boy," called Laird Ruthven, "come join me at the table and tell me everything."

"Aye, laird," he answered, thinking this was more punishment than reward until he realized that Vida was at the table too.

He spent the biggest part of the next hour recounting every detail of the night's events to Ambrose Ruthven, who listened with something akin to awe.

When he reached the part where he decided to let the men go, Ambrose frowned.

"I don't like the fact that Gow was thieving from me. You should have run them through, tied them to their horses, and sent them home. That would have sent a message."

Tomas nodded as if agreeing. Obviously Ambrose never gave a thought to the consequences of acting hastily. "I understand, Laird. Believe me, I would have liked nothing more. But as I considered things, I realized that isn't the message ye would have wanted to send. I'm sure ye know it would have infuriated Gow and he'd have to seek vengeance for their lives. With the current state of things, we might not be able to withstand that kind of attack. But I knew ye'd want him dealt with nonetheless. Ye can be sure, he received a valuable message this way. In the face of their thievery, ye will be seen to have been generous. His men weren't injured—except perhaps for their pride. The matter was kept quiet and Gow lost a bit less than he would have if ye'd asked a ransom. But most important, he knows ye're not the soft target he thought ye were. And that is a message we want spread around."

Ambrose frowned. "I see your point. He has absolutely nothing to be angry about."

"Exactly."

Ambrose's eyes narrowed and he appeared to be considering what Tomas had said. "I wouldn't have thought of that."

No, of course ye wouldn't have, ye vengeful bastard.

"You've an excellent head on your shoulders, Tomas. Every day I'm more impressed."

"Thank ye, laird." He glanced at Vida who had been listening quietly to the tale.

She gave him the smile he was beginning to crave. The one so full of warmth and light. It fired the heat in his belly.

"You've been a blessing to us," she said, and a faint blush pinked her cheeks. That bit of shyness just increased her allure.

"Aye, that's precisely it. A blessing." Echoed her father. "I can never thank you or Laird Carr sufficiently. But now, young man, you've earned a rest."

"Aye. I'll just finish breaking my fast, then I'll go to the barracks." After their second night there, the laird had found sleeping quarters for them with the other Ruthven warriors.

"Nay, lad, yesterday I decided the three of you deserve to have private quarters. I've had a room in the keep prepared for you. Vida, my sweet, would you show Sir Tomas to the new accommodations after he's eaten his fill?"

"Aye, Papa, certainly."

"Now, if you'll excuse me. I quite enjoy watching the men train these days." And with that, Ambrose left the table.

"Thank you, Tomas," Vida said softly.

"No more thanks are necessary. Once we've been likened to a gift from God, there's not much more to say." He winked at her

She laughed. "True, but I'm thanking you for something else."

"I can't imagine what."

She let out a deep sigh. "You haven't been here long and since you have, my father has been in a very good mood. However, he has always been quick to release his wrath. Years ago, I found that I could temper his responses some. I think he didn't like to reveal his darker side to me. As a result, at least when I'm around, he doesn't get so uncontrollably angry."

Tomas frowned. He hadn't yet seen the truly awful side of Ruthven that he remembered, but neither had he realized it was Vida who was responsible for that.

Perhaps reading his expression, she hastened to clarify. "Don't get me wrong. He has mellowed since he was a younger man. Everybody says so. But in very bad situations, he is more likely to slip into old patterns. That's one reason I went with him to Dundee."

"I don't understand."

"Papa has invested quite a bit in two ships bound for Mediterranean ports, and he's had no word of them. I fear if something goes awry, he'll be furious."

"Do ye have some reason to think something went awry?"

"Not precisely. The *Mermaid Queen* was bound for Genoa and the *Merry Mistress* for Venice. We didn't expect the *Mermaid Queen* before Michaelmas and perhaps not until the end of November. The *Merry Mistress* isn't likely to return until Epiphany or later. He wasn't worried until he heard of another ship bound for Genoa which left port several days after the *Mermaid Queen* and has since returned."

"And your father's hasn't?"

"Nay. As yet, there's no cause to worry. The captain of each vessel must sell the goods he carries and use those funds to purchase goods with which to return. He might have taken longer to do that or simply pushed for better trading terms. A small delay is worth it if the journey is more profitable overall and Papa's captains drive hard bargains. But I went with him to Dundee, just in case he needed my help. As you saw today, when he's angry, he overreacts. Had he been there last night, instead of you, and without me, he would have done exactly as he threatened."

Tomas shook his head. "That would have been a disaster. I wouldn't have been surprised to see the Gows riding on Cotharach tomorrow had we done that."

"Aye, you know that. So do I. And the truth is Papa does too, because it is exactly what he would have done if the situation were reversed. But in the heat of the moment, he would have lost sight of the consequences. Last night you acted with a clear head and fair retribution. And on top of that, the way you explained it, made it easier for Papa to hear. He didn't feel ye were criticizing or contradicting him. In fact, ye convinced him he would have made exactly the same wise choices and that Gow will attribute those choices to him. For that, Tomas, I am deeply grateful."

Tomas chuckled.

She smiled. "What amuses you?"

He shrugged. "I guess I didn't realize it at the time, but I did exactly what my mother does when she wants my da to see things her way. She makes him think it was his idea. She's always called it, 'going around to the postern gate.'"

Vida laughed. In Tomas's opinion, there was no more beautiful sound.

"I think I'd like your mother. Perhaps I can meet her someday."

Tomas sobered. That wasn't likely to ever happen. "She rarely leaves the Highlands, but I'm sure ye'd like her." Tomas was absolutely certain of that. His mother would adore her young cousin.

"Well, maybe someday. For now, you look exhausted. Let me show you to your new quarters."

He followed her out of the hall, up two flights of stairs. "Yer ankle appears to be completely healed."

"Aye. It only pained me for the first few days. I used the walking stick for several more so as not to reinjure it. But it's perfectly fine now."

She led him down a corridor, opened a chamber door and stood back to let him enter.

"Sir Drew's chamber is across the hall and Sir Ethan has been given the one next door."

He was a little surprised. Somehow, he'd assumed they'd all been given one room. Ruthven must be feeling very generous indeed. Tomas stepped into the well-appointed chamber. It was on the east side of the keep and thus was flooded with the morning light.

"This is very nice. Thank ye."

"I'm glad you like it."

"I'm sure it will be most comfortable."

"I hope so. I'll go and let you rest now, but before I do, I was just wondering...never mind. Have a good rest."

"What were ye wondering, lass?"

Her cheeks blushed crimson and she wouldn't meet his gaze. "I was just wondering if you'd play chess with me again tonight."

He grinned, but looking down as she was, she couldn't have seen it. "I'd love to."

She glanced up at him briefly, rewarding him with her radiant smile. "Good. I will see ye later then." She started to leave, but stopped as if she wanted to say more.

"Is there something else?"

"Aye. Well…it's just…I mean…well…I'm glad you were one of the men who decided to stay."

Almost before he realized what she said, the door was closed and she was gone. He grinned. He'd have given nearly anything to see the blush that surely stained her cheeks after that comment.

CHAPTER 7

Tomas was very pleased when after the first few weeks, all of the Ruthven men had been trained in how best to patrol the holding to prevent raiders. That meant he, Drew, and Ethan no longer had to ride out at night and could focus on building each warrior's skills. They were having mixed results with that and they retired early one evening to discuss it privately, gathering in Tomas's room which was slightly bigger and contained a table and four chairs.

They had barely made themselves comfortable when there was a knock at the door. Tomas opened it to a serving maid, bearing a jug of wine, goblets, a plate of sliced apples, pears, and cheese, and what appeared to be a small loaf of nut-bread. It had always been one of his favorites.

"Moyna bid me to bring these up to you."

"Thank ye, lass. Just put the tray on the table and please give Moyna my thanks as well." Tomas felt a bit guilty. He'd wanted the opportunity to speak with Moyna alone, but the few times he'd tried during the day, there had been too many people around.

He knew the best chance he had of catching her alone would be to seek her out in the kitchen an hour or more after supper. By then, things would be cleaned up and most of the serving women would be gone. When Tomas lived here as a child, Moyna stayed in a small room off the kitchen. It had apparently been her home ever since her husband had died. Tomas doubted that had changed.

Unfortunately, when a certain green-eyed lass captured his attention in the evening, all thoughts of Moyna fled. He vowed to make a point of seeing her very soon.

"What's made ye go quiet?" asked Ethan.

Tomas shrugged. "Nothing really. I need to try to speak with Moyna alone. She clearly remembers me and hasn't said anything. She is surrounded by servants and occupied until well after the evening meal."

Drew grinned. "And by that time, ye're so enraptured with Lady Vida that ye forget the old cook even exists."

"I'm not enraptured with Vida."

"No?" asked Ethan. "Then do ye mind if I pay her court?"

Tomas scowled. Yes, he minded. He minded quite a lot.

"Cool yer temper, friend," added Ethan. "I'm jesting. She only has eyes for ye anyway."

Tomas shook his head. "Nay, that's not true. We're just friends. She likes to play chess and no one else is willing to lose constantly."

Drew laughed. "Keep telling yerself that. But the truth is, she's fallen hard and fast for ye."

Tomas's scowl deepened. "Nay, she hasn't. At least, she'd better not have."

"And why's that?" Asked Ethan.

"Because she'll get hurt. I don't love her. I can't love her. We aren't staying here, remember? We leave in February, if not sooner."

Ethan chuckled. "Tomas, ye care for her and ye're deluding yerself if ye think ye don't. There's no question in my mind that she's fond of ye. What's more, her papa thinks ye hung the moon."

Tomas rolled his eyes. "He might, but that doesn't mean he'd want me to marry his daughter. And I sure as hell don't want that bastard for a father-in-law. Nay, we have a specific mission. Bring the Ruthven soldiers' skills up to a satisfactory level to ensure the clan is protected. That's it. And to that, our plan tonight was to discuss what our next steps are—not the Lady Vida's romantic notions."

They did discuss their plans late into the night. They identified a handful of men who had been sufficiently talented to start with and who had already learned a great deal. These men had the potential to become the very best in the clan and Tomas believed it was most important to work closely with them to assure this. "When we leave, we must have a group of highly skilled men who can take over training and continue to build the other men's skills."

They also identified a few men who needed intense, focused training, or they would be a liability forever. Most of the rest were doing well enough with the training they were currently being given. Only after they had their next steps completely mapped out did they retire for the night.

When Tomas finally lay on his bed, he was exhausted and ready to sleep, and yet sleep eluded him. His mind kept replaying the things Drew and Ethan had said about Vida…*she's fallen hard and fast for ye…ye care for her and ye're deluding yerself if ye think ye don't*. He couldn't do this.

He couldn't have her.

He didn't want her.

As he thought about her sweet personality, her breathtaking smile, her enchanting laughter, and her sheer beauty, he knew instantly that thought was blatantly false. His increasing hardness told him he absolutely wanted her. He had never desired any woman so completely. But his desires could not be allowed to cloud his judgement. Vida Ruthven was not a woman he could have.

A very, very evil part of him whispered, *what better revenge for the horrible things Ruthven had done than to steal his daughter's innocence before returning to the Highlands?* But he shut that down immediately. It probably would destroy Ruthven if he learned his former stable boy had despoiled his daughter. Nevertheless, the person most hurt would be Vida. Tomas could never allow that to happen. Why? Because Ethan was right, Tomas cared for her. More than that, he *liked* her. He enjoyed simply being with her. In fact, he looked forward to the time they spent together at meals, or playing chess in the evening.

He also admired her. She lost her mother at a very young age, but she had apparently managed to rein in her father's temper from early on. He realized she now played the exact same role his mother had played in the clan. Only where Katherine could only protect others from Ruthven's anger by seeing it directed towards her, Vida had the ability to calm her father simply with her presence. His mother would completely adore her.

But the fact remained he couldn't have Vida Ruthven. As much as he desired her, he could not imagine staying here. Nay, it was out of the question. Still, perhaps he wouldn't have to. Maybe he could talk her into returning to the Highlands with him. Laird Carr had even suggested that if the Ruthven garrison didn't show sufficient improvement by February, Lady Vida should be removed to the Highlands for her own safety. Maybe, even if the Ruthven men had improved, Tomas could convince her father that they didn't have sufficient skills yet and he would see the wisdom in sending her away. That could be the very sweetest revenge possible. By all indications, Ruthven had hated Katherine. He had no compunction about sending her to the Highlands in order to steal her lands and title. Maybe Tomas could take Ruthven's beloved daughter away to the Highlands, leaving him with only the lands and title he so coveted.

Even as he considered this, he knew she wouldn't go willingly. Just as his mother hadn't wanted to leave her people. But there was no sense worrying about it now. He'd cross that bridge when he came to it. Maybe this would be possible.

~ * ~

Vida had been disappointed when Tomas and the other Carr men excused themselves from the hall right after supper. Playing chess with him in the evening had become the thing she looked most forward to every day. Tomas was funny and smart. He was an excellent chess player and he made the game truly a challenge. What he'd said about learning different things from different people was true. She had improved her own game by playing with him and he seemed to be learning from her. She had nearly lost several times, but she hadn't been tempted again to throw the game. He liked that she challenged him. And she liked that she didn't have to pretend with him.

Vida was quickly coming to realize there was much more to it than simply enjoying the game. She could no longer deny her growing attraction. She'd never experienced this before. When she was with him, it felt as if a flock of twittering birds took flight in her belly.

He didn't treat her like any other man of her acquaintance.

Of course, she didn't have much experience with other men. When in the company of lowland nobility, her father was never more than an arm's length away. Oh, she had met many noblemen and she had no doubt that any number of them would have jumped at the opportunity to negotiate a betrothal with her father. But very few of them ever spoke a word to her other than a polite greeting.

Then there were her clansmen. To them she was always "Lady Vida." They would never have spoken to her in anything less than a formal, respectful manner. She could at least have a conversation with Father Michael or her papa, but that was the extent of her experience with men.

Tomas MacHenry was another story entirely. He talked with her and asked questions as if he truly wanted her opinion. He would laugh with her and tease her. He made subtle innuendos that could make her blush even as the yearning to discover the things he hinted at burned inside her. He looked at her in a way that suggested he might desire her too and that made her feel beautiful.

She felt alive when she was with him in a way she never had before. To Tomas, she wasn't a noblewoman to be treated with care, or a possible bride with whom a betrothal might be negotiated. She was a woman. A woman whose company he enjoyed and whom he found attractive.

As Emma had helped her get ready for bed that night, Vida was still pre-occupied with thoughts of Tomas.

"What on earth has you so distracted, my lady? You haven't heard a thing I've said to you."

"I'm sorry, Emma, did you say something?"

Emma laughed. "No, but that just goes to show how far away your head is. Or is it not so far away after all? Perhaps it's upstairs with a certain handsome young Highlander."

Vida smiled, knowing her face had gone red. "He is rather attractive, isn't he?"

"Oh yes, Sir Ethan's a fine specimen of a man."

"Ethan? I wasn't thinking about Ethan."

Emma laughed harder. "I know you're not thinking about Ethan. By the saints my lady, 'tis obviously Sir Tomas you're pining for."

"I'm not pining."

"Nay? You've been down in the mouth all evening— ever since they retired early."

"Was I that obvious? Does everyone know?"

"Everyone knows you like him. Except perhaps your father, and he's too enamored with Sir Tomas himself to pay attention to what you think of our guest."

Vida grinned. "Papa does seem to be rather impressed with him."

Emma sobered. "Aye, he does. But Lady Vida, don't get caught up in a fantasy. As much as your father likes him, he isn't a nobleman and I suspect Laird Ruthven's affection will fall short of allowing you to marry Sir Tomas. Besides which, the Carrs will only be here until February at the latest."

"They could stay longer…"

"Nay, Lady Vida, don't count on that. It's fine to enjoy Sir Tomas's company while he's here, but don't let it go further. In that way lies heart ache."

"You worry too much, Emma. I know everything you say is true. I'll be careful with my heart. I swear I will."

Now Vida lay in bed, still thinking of her handsome Highlander, being anything but careful. She imagined what it would be like to be kissed by him, to be held close and loved. To marry him. She didn't care what Emma had said, there wasn't a man anywhere in Scotland who would be a better leader for this clan. If she could just get her papa to see that, she might have a hope. Surely, if Sir Tomas were offered a title and lands, he would consider staying here as her husband.

Emma was right about Papa, though. Sir Tomas, the warrior who was helping to train the Ruthven garrison, was worthy of the adoration of men. But where her hand in marriage was concerned, her papa wouldn't be as accepting.

What was it Tomas had said about what his mother did when she wanted his da to see things her way? *She makes him think it was his idea. She's always called it 'going around to the postern gate.'* That was it. Maybe Vida could find a *postern gate* and make Papa think it was his idea. She'd have to keep her eyes open.

CHAPTER 8

Vida had been looking forward to the feast of All Saints for days. It would be the first holy day celebration they'd had since the Carr warriors had arrived. She wanted everything to be perfect and for their guests to enjoy themselves. But most of all, she wanted to dance with Tomas.

She loved to dance, but had only ever done so with her father, Father Michael, and a few of her father's men who were careful not to overstep their bounds. But she'd always imagined what dancing with a man she desired would be like. Being so close, touching hands, gazing into each other's eyes. She imagined feeling inextricably joined, if only for a few moments, by the music and the rhythmic flow of the dance. She closed her eyes and sighed. She reckoned dancing could be one of the most intimate things a couple could do in public.

"Lady Vida?" The steward interrupted her musings.

She opened her eyes. "Aye, Manus. Do you need something?"

"We are nearly ready to start the feast, but your father went out to the courtyard with Sir Tomas some time ago. Since the other men were given the holiday off from training, the laird thought to have some time alone to improve his skills."

Vida smiled and shook her head. "Poor Sir Tomas wasn't given the same courtesy as the other men. What do you wish me to do?"

"About a half hour ago, I went out to tell the laird the feast was almost ready and he nearly chewed the face off of me for interrupting. I thought perhaps you might have better luck."

"Aye, of course. I'll go get him." She crossed to the front doors looking back once at the hall before leaving. It was perfect. Candles were being lit against the late afternoon gloom and everything seemed to glitter in the light. She smiled, walked through the entryway, and out of the keep. A gust of wind instantly chilled her and catching her sheer veil, caused it to fly out behind her. She wore a cream-colored linen kirtle under a burgundy brocade gown, which the biting cold penetrated instantly. She probably should have fetched a mantle, but there seemed little point now. She would only be out here for a few minutes.

She hurried down the steps and across the courtyard to where her father was sparring with Tomas. "Papa," she called but they didn't hear her. She continued closer and called again. Still they didn't hear. She was almost upon them when Tomas heard her call, and stopped the match.

Her father looked up. "Good heavens, child, what are you doing out here?"

"Papa, the feast is nearly ready. I didn't think you would want our guests left waiting."

"Oh, right. Yes, we should get back to the keep." He turned and headed across the courtyard.

She shivered. "Aye, we should."

Tomas scowled. "Ye're freezing. Ye should never have come out without a cloak. Here, I'll wrap my plaid around ye 'til we get back to the keep." He held it out with one arm.

She only hesitated a moment before stepping close and allowing him to wrap an arm and his blanket-like cloak around her. She was instantly enveloped in warmth. *Holy Mother of God.* Could anything on earth feel as wonderful as this?

"Now, let's get ye inside."

He walked with her at his side until they reached the doors. It was much too short a walk. A mile would have been too short a walk. Once inside, he stepped away from her and gone was the glorious connection between them forged as he shared his warmth with her.

"There now, go on into the hall, near the fire. And don't venture out so lightly dressed again." He paused to look at her, and as if really seeing her for the first time, stared intently with an undeniable hunger in his gaze. He added, "Not that I minded having my arm around ye. I think I could get used to that."

What the things he said did to her. She must be crimson. How did one respond to that? *Me too?* "I...I..."

He laughed. "Go on into the hall."

"Where are you going?"

"I'm just going to wash up. I'll be down in a few minutes." But he made no move to step away from her.

"Don't be long," she said and then kissed him.

She did it without thinking. It just seemed like the thing to do. She put a hand on his chest, stood on her tiptoes, and kissed him. It was a quick, innocent kiss and it had even shocked her, so the stunned look on Tomas's face should have come as no surprise.

But she was horrified when she realized what she'd just done. Her hands flew to her mouth and she turned to flee. Before she had taken more than a step, he caught her upper arm in one hand and pulled her with him into the relative seclusion of the stairwell.

"Let's try that again, shall we?" He slipped his hand behind her neck, leaned down, and kissed her. There was absolutely nothing innocent about his kiss. He held her to him and nudged her mouth open, sucking on her lower lip before dipping his tongue into her mouth.

When he was finished, she was breathless. And speechless. She just stared up at him.

He grinned and kissed her again. Then he winked as said, "Anything worth doing, is worth doing right. Wouldn't ye agree?"

"Oh...aye," she said without thinking.

He chuckled. "I'll be down in a few minutes. I won't be long. Trust me." He turned and jogged up the stairs.

She wasn't sure how long she'd stood there gaping, but eventually she came to her senses, straightened her veil, and went into the great hall.

The rest of the night could be a total disaster and she wouldn't care. His kiss had been the single most exhilarating moment of her life and nothing would spoil that.

But the rest of the night wasn't a disaster. It was magical. He sat with her during the feast and then danced with her most of the evening. And dancing with him was everything she imagined it would be and more. For the first time in her life, she wasn't focused on all of her responsibilities. She was vaguely aware that a messenger had arrived, and she should have made certain he was fed and had a place to sleep for the night. But then again, if she didn't, someone else would. The only thing that mattered for her was the enchantment of the celebration. Oh, and the feel of his lips on hers as he stole another kiss before retiring for the night.

~ * ~

Ambrose paced his solar. The feast of All Saints continued in his great hall, but he was no longer in the mood to celebrate. He had slipped away from the fete shortly after the messenger from Naughton Lindsay arrived.

He should probably force a smile and go back down. Vida was bound to notice his absence and come looking for him. But he could not tell her about this. Nor could he return to the feast as if nothing had happened.

He picked up the message and read it again.

Ambrose, by the grace of God, Laird of Clan Ruthven,

I hope this missive finds you well and hearty and that Clan Ruthven enjoyed a bountiful harvest this year.

I fear it is unseemly for me to raise this issue, but alas, I must address your outstanding debt. You have remained silent on the matter thus far, but it has been brought to my attention that the Mermaid Queen has not yet returned. As the loan I graciously extended to you was guaranteed with that cargo, I am forced to consider the alternate form of payment we discussed, namely a betrothal to your daughter, Davida.

I have taken the liberty of having a betrothal agreement drafted and it is enclosed. If you wish to negotiate the terms of the agreement, I would most happily meet with you in your Dundee shipping office before the end of the month on the date of your choosing.

Sincerely,

Naughton Lindsay

Ambrose could scarcely believe what he was reading. *Alternate form of payment? A betrothal agreement?* He had not guaranteed the loan with his daughter's hand. That had just been a jest Naughton made. He hadn't agreed to it. He would never, ever, willingly marry his precious Vida to a man like Naughton Lindsay and he'd send him a scathing letter telling him so.

He went to his desk, pulled out parchment, quill, and ink, and started writing.

To Naughton, Godforsaken, Lindsay,

You have taken leave of your senses if you think I would marry my daughter to filth like you. I never agreed to a betrothal and I never will.

I agreed to repay your loan, with interest, when the Mermaid Queen returned or by the end of December and nothing compels me to do so earlier.

I have enclosed the ashes of your farcical betrothal. Don't insult me by ever suggesting such a preposterous notion again!

Ambrose, Laird of Clan Ruthven

He sat, reading and rereading it. He burned the betrothal, folded his message around the ashes, and affixed his seal. This would certainly send the ignorant upstart a message. He was almost to the door of his solar, prepared to give it to the messenger and send him on his way, when he stopped. He remembered what Sir Tomas had said after Ambrose suggested it would have been better to kill the Gow raiders. "Believe me, I would have liked nothing more. But as I considered things, I realized that isn't the message ye would have wanted to send." Tomas had been certain killing the men would have infuriated Gow and forced him to seek vengeance.

"I don't care if the steaming pile of shite seeks vengeance. Let him try."

But he also had to concede Tomas had been right about another thing. Although improving, the Ruthvens were not prepared to withstand an attack from the likes of Clan Lindsay.

He looked at the letter in his hands. As good as it had felt to write it and as much as he'd like to send it, he knew it would be utter folly. Sighing heavily, he tossed the sealed letter into the hearth and watched as the hungry flames consumed it. Then he sat and stared at his desk, not sure what to write, but knowing a response was necessary. Finally, he picked up his quill again.

> *To Naughton Lindsay,*
>
> *I am well and I hope you are the same. The Ruthven harvest was adequate, thank you for asking.*
>
> *As to my debt to you, I have only "remained silent" because my ships have not yet returned from the Mediterranean. As we agreed, I intend to repay the loan when the Mermaid Queen returns or by the end of December. I give you my pledge as a gentleman that I will honor this agreement.*
>
> *I will contact you as soon as one of these eventualities occur.*
>
> *Ambrose, Laird of Clan Ruthven*

He didn't mention the betrothal. It didn't bear consideration.

This letter hadn't given him nearly the satisfaction of the first, but it was the prudent course. He folded and sealed the letter. He'd give it to the messenger before the man left in the morning.

Still not wishing to return to the celebration, he went to bed. As he lay staring at the ceiling, he realized his anger at Lindsay had obscured the real issue at hand. He had a massive debt coming due, and his ship really should have returned by now. If it didn't return before the end of December, he would have to repay Lindsay from the funds he had available. Perhaps he could renegotiate the terms. Maybe Lindsay would take half at the end of December and agree to accept the remainder, with additional interest, when the ship bound for Venice returned.

Ambrose eventually fell into a fitful sleep haunted by terrible dreams. He dreamed the light of his life, his Vida, was being dragged away from the keep by Naughton Lindsay. She cried and begged her papa for help, but he couldn't seem to move. He called orders to his men to stop Lindsay, but they too seemed frozen, unable to act. He called for Tomas. Tomas would save her as he had before…only Tomas didn't come. He woke from that nightmare in a panic, calling for Tomas.

After what seemed like hours, he was finally able get back to sleep, only to find himself locked in another nightmare. This time raiders were attacking relentlessly, he was losing everything and nothing he or his men tried to do would stop them. He needed Tomas. Tomas would know what to do. He called for him over and over. The dream Gregor said, "He's gone, Laird. Gone. Gone home."

Then the dream shifted and it wasn't raiders he fought, but a clan laying siege. They battered the gates and the walls and his castle crumbled around him. This time, his men could fight. They fought for all they were worth, but one by one they were cut down. Everyone he knew lay dead around him. He was the last person left to shield Vida and he couldn't do it. He was shoved aside as men grabbed his precious daughter. He could only lay there, surrounded by his dead clansmen, and listen to his daughter's screams as the attackers carried her away.

He awoke drenched in sweat and sobbing.

Once he managed to get a hold of himself, he considered everything that had occurred in his nightmares and landed on one truth. He needed Sir Tomas. Not just to train his men and not just until February. He needed him to stay forever as the captain of his guard, the commander of his men. In the dark, cold hours before dawn, he vowed to do whatever it took to convince Tomas to stay.

~ * ~

For Tomas, the evening of All Saints had been wonderful from the instant he'd first seen Vida walking across the courtyard—her veil flying behind her, her hair tousled by the wind, and her cheeks pink with cold—to the moments their lips parted as they said goodnight. That she had made the first move earlier in the evening, with her chaste kiss, stunned and delighted him.

Of course, the attention he'd paid to her all evening hadn't gone unnoticed. Drew and Ethan had both felt the need to remind him of the folly in this, but he didn't care. He would deal with the consequences when they occurred and no sooner.

The next morning, he went downstairs early, hoping to see Vida, but to his chagrin it was Ambrose who awaited him.

God's bones, he hadn't expected to have to deal with the consequences this quickly.

"Good morning, Laird. Ye're up earlier than usual." He kept his tone light.

Ambrose nodded, almost distractedly. "Aye. I didn't sleep well. There's something I'd like to discuss with you."

"Ah. I see." Tomas sat down. He would not stand before the man to receive an upbraiding, like an errant child. "What concerns ye?"

"Oh, I don't want to talk about it here. Break your fast, lad, then we'll go to my solar."

"I'm not overly hungry. We can talk about this first, if ye wish."

"Aye, that's probably best. Follow me."

Once they had reached the solar, Ambrose invited him to sit in one of the upholstered chairs near the hearth.

"I…well…this is rather difficult."

"If I've done something—"

"Oh, good heavens, no. I guess I'll just dive in. Tomas, I can't tell you what the time ye've spent with me means. I don't suppose ye can understand this, or maybe ye can. I've never asked about yer parents. But I was a younger son my entire life. Leadership was meant for Ainsley. My father focused all of his energies on his oldest son. I guess I understand how that can happen. Perhaps if I'd had a son after Vida was born, he would have been my sole focus."

Here it comes. The stay-away-from-my-daughter speech.

Ambrose paused, appearing lost in thought. "Still, I'd like to think not. Vida is precious to me—no less precious than a son would have been. I could have loved them both."

Part of Tomas doubted that. The Ambrose Ruthven he knew nineteen years ago didn't seem like the kind of man to value a daughter. And yet, he clearly did now.

"The fact remains that I was not my father's priority. I realize now I could have pushed to learn the same things, but I didn't. I felt slighted and decided to learn other skills. I invested small sums in shipping. And as that turned to profit, I'd invest more. I was good at it and, eventually, I convinced myself that becoming a wealthy man in my own right was better than becoming the laird of the clan."

"I can understand that." This was not at all what Tomas was expecting.

"But the thing that none of us had considered was what would happen if Ainsley died. My father simply assumed he'd be the heir and his children after him. But Ainsley did die, leaving only a child of ten and three, a daughter. I was faced with years of leading a clan in her name. Not only was it something I hadn't been trained to do, but I would never reap the benefits. The title of Laird Ruthven would pass to her *husband*."

It required supreme effort for Tomas not to react to this.

"Still, there was more to it than most people knew. I had fallen in love with a woman, and she with me, but her laird wouldn't agree to the union."

Tomas thought that probably wasn't a bad decision.

"Ainsley believed he would never marry again and would thus never have a son. In an attempt to make the betrothal, he offered to stipulate that if Moibeal and I had a son, the title of Laird of Clan Ruthven would pass to me and then him." Ruthven shook his head as if in disbelief. "I was astounded. No other man I know would have done that. But it didn't make a difference. Have you ever been in love, Tomas?"

"I…uh…I don't think so." Images of Vida flashed through his mind. He liked her and was attracted to her. She was smart and funny and very beautiful, but did he love her? Surely not. He couldn't love her, could he? Then images from the night before swirled around his mind and the reality of it crashed in on him. *Damnation.* He did love her, but he certainly wouldn't admit that to her father. "No, sir. I…I've never been in love."

"Well, I cannot describe the pain of loving someone, of knowing they love you, and then see them married to someone else. It damn near killed me."

Tomas felt an unwelcome twinge of pity.

"Then, within a month of her wedding, Ainsley died. Had her uncle allowed us to marry, we would have become laird and lady of the clan. If we'd had a son, he would have inherited the title on my death. If we didn't, my niece and her husband would have. But none of that was to be. I inherited the guardianship of a willful girl and all the weighty responsibilities of a clan without the title."

And there it was, the reason Tomas didn't feel sorry for Ambrose.

"A few years later, Moibeal's husband died and she was free to marry again, but I still needed the title to get her laird to agree. I sought King David's help. He found a man with lands and a title of his own who would marry my niece and forfeit her lands and title in exchange for a larger dowry in gold. It was the perfect solution for everyone and I was finally able to marry the woman I loved."

"What happened to yer niece?" Tomas asked, barely controlling his anger. "Do ye even know?"

"Oh, yes. Moibeal was concerned about her, so I looked into things. I understand she is very happy."

"Ye weren't concerned?"

"Of course not. King David wouldn't have married her to a monster and her husband seemed like a decent man. He's a Highland laird. Perhaps you've heard of him, Niall MacIan, Laird of Clan MacIan."

"Aye, the MacIans and the Carrs are allies."

Ambrose smiled broadly. "Then you must know my niece. She's Lady Katherine MacIan."

"Aye, we've met. She's a fine lady. Well loved and respected by her clan."

"It's good to hear she's no longer the spoiled, willful child she once was."

White hot anger boiled up in Tomas. He didn't trust himself to speak so he remained silent.

"I've digressed. This was all just to say that I never really learned the things Ainsley did. It was Moibeal and then Vida who took on the management of the clan while I was building my business. I'd never had the opportunity to learn the skills of a warrior, either. And I guess, by extension, I didn't know what my men needed to learn. But you are a gifted young man. A natural born leader and my admiration for you grows daily."

"Thank ye." *Where in hell was this going?*

"Tomas, I don't want you to return to Laird Carr in February."

"I'm sorry, Laird. I must."

"Please hear me out. I'm not just asking you to stay a little longer and help train my men. I'm asking you to stay forever. I want you to be my commander. My right hand. The leader of my men and protector of my clan."

Tomas was stunned. "Well…I…uh…didn't see this coming." Part of him wanted to laugh loud and long in the old man's face before revealing who he really was and refusing the offer. But another part of him thought about Vida. As repugnant has Tomas found Ambrose, Vida loved her father and hurting him would hurt her.

"Will you do it? Will you accept my offer? I'll pay you handsomely. You'll be a rich man in your own right."

Hell no, was on the tip of Tomas's tongue, but instead he said, "I don't know…my home is in the Highlands."

"Please Tomas, I'm begging you, please at least consider my offer."

Tomas inclined his head for a moment before saying, "I'll consider it," even though he had absolutely no intention of accepting the offer.

CHAPTER 9

Tomas left Ambrose's solar after making the ridiculous promise to consider becoming commander of the Ruthven garrison. Why had he done that? Laughing the old man out of the room wouldn't have been the correct choice, but agreeing to consider the proposal probably wasn't right either. He was going to have to say no and the sooner the better.

He made his way down the stairs. Although he intended to go to the great hall, he realized Vida would be there. With so much on his mind, he thought it better to stay away from that which addled his senses the most. He turned and went out of the keep. He still hadn't had the chance to speak with Moyna alone and now was the perfect time. He needed to talk to someone who knew who he really was, and who would appreciate the predicament he was in. Drew and Ethan would agree with him that he should flatly refuse Ruthven's offer, and leave. But Moyna would understand.

He strode around the outside of the keep to the side where the kitchens were. He stepped into the main kitchen and was met with the usual bustle of activity.

"Sir Tomas," exclaimed one of the lasses as she looked up from her work, a huge smile spreading across her face.

Several other women also turned and greeted him.

Moyna, too, stopped her work. "Good morning, Sir Tomas, what brings you to the kitchens?"

"Good morning, Moyna. Actually, I was hoping I could have a word with ye."

"Certainly, ye can." She wiped her hands on her apron before removing it and stepping out of the kitchen. Once outside, she said, "I've been wanting to have a private chat with ye as well, but privacy is hard to come by around here."

He smiled and nodded. "Aye, it is."

"Let's step into the chapel. 'Twill be private and out of the wind."

Once inside the privacy of the chapel, she turned and opened her arms to him. "Now, my sweet wee lad, give me a hug."

He wrapped his arms around her. His life here had been hard, but a few people had made it better. Of course, Father James, Manus, and a few others had treated him well. But next to Katherine, Moyna had been the kindest of all.

"You've grown into a fine man, Tomas. I nearly dropped the tray I was carrying when I first saw you."

"How did ye know it was me? I've changed a wee bit."

She laughed, "Aye, more than a wee bit. But I knew yer da when he was a young man. Handsome he was, although too young for me. You're the image of him."

"Then do others know too?"

Moyna chuckled. "Aye, some of the older women do and for the same reason. At some point in their youth, they'd all hoped to catch your da's eye. Of course, Manus recognized ye too, but like everyone else, he has no intention of letting on."

"Give them my thanks. It's probably best this way."

"Aye, I expect so. What you're doing for the clan is simply wonderful. No one wants anything to interfere with that. Now, come sit down and tell me your story. When you went missing, we all knew what had happened. Laird Ruthven ranted and railed about it for hours." She imitated the laird's manner, "How dare he take my servant? He owes me. I have a notion to ride and take back what's mine."

"Ye're jesting. He didn't give a flea's fart about me, except that I was someone he could vent his wrath on."

"Aye, ye're right there, but he needed something to blow on about. Finally, after he'd calmed a little, Manus reminded him that you, your father, and your grandfather were freemen and not serfs. Thus, even as a wee lad, ye had every right to go. But we never learned what happened after that. How is it you came to be a Carr? 'Twas Laird MacIan that took Lady Katherine."

"Moyna, I'm not a Carr. Lady Katherine and Laird MacIan adopted me. They raised me as their own son. My name is Tomas MacIan."

"Then, why were you with the Carrs?"

"When we have to deliver taxes to the crown, we usually join with several of our allies to guard against thieves. Of the men who were with us, only five were Laird Carr's men. One man, Quinn MacKenzie, represented Laird MacLennan. Sir Drew and four of the men were his. I represented my father and the other five, including Sir Ethan, were MacIan men."

"You're the son of a Highland laird and Lady Katherine is your mama. Your parents and your grandda would be so proud of you."

"I'm glad ye think so. That makes me happy."

"How is Lady Katherine?"

Tomas grinned. "Blissfully happy. She has loved Da from the first days and he believes the sun rises and sets for her. They have three children. A daughter, Beitris, who is about Vida's age, and two sons. James is fifteen and Alex is twelve."

Moyna bowed her head in prayer. "Thank you, God." When she looked up, she added, "I've remembered her in my prayers every day."

"I know she has always kept everyone here in her prayers as well. Her heart broke having to leave. And she damn near died before Da got her home. The lashes on her back festered." He looked away. "That was my fault."

"What are you talking about?"

"He beat her because she was trying to save me."

"He beat her because he was an angry, bitter man. And as bad as you feel, how bad do you think she'd have felt if she'd let him continue beating you? You would have died. Would you want her suffering that guilt?"

"Nay, I don't suppose so. I'd never thought of it that way."

"Then, it's time you start. You both lived and thrived and that's what's important."

He couldn't argue the point. "Aye, that's true."

"So, no more talk of it's being anyone's fault but the laird's."

"It's still hard to think of how he treated her. But, speaking of him, this morning he told me his story about why he wanted the Ruthven title and lands."

Moyna nodded. "Aye, in sending Lady Katherine off to the Highlands, he did get his heart's desire. He married Moibeal Dundas and she was a perfectly lovely woman. She was kind and compassionate and just as Vida does now, she could temper his anger. He has mellowed considerably."

Tomas frowned. He wasn't sure how to ask what he wanted to know.

"You don't believe he's mellowed?"

"Nay, it's not that. I have seen it with my own eyes."

"But something is bothering you?"

"Aye. I guess I'm a little surprised that Lady Katherine has been forgotten. One of my first evenings here, Vida told me her uncle Ainsley died with no children."

Moyna sighed. "Aye, Lady Vida believes that, but it doesn't mean we've forgotten Lady Katherine. As soon as it became evident to the laird that he was going to be able to marry Lady Moibeal, he forbade anyone to mention Lady Katherine ever again. Mind you, Lady Moibeal had met Katherine years before and knew that the king had arranged a marriage for her. But she didn't know all of the circumstances and Laird Ruthven didn't fill in the details. He

96

allowed Lady Moibeal to believe that Lady Katherine *wanted* to marry Laird MacIan as much as the king wanted them married. The laird threatened us with our lives if we ever disavowed her of that notion. So, because we were never to mention Lady Katherine, by the time Lady Vida was old enough to understand anything, she had never heard anyone speak of her cousin. I expect if her mother had lived, she might have told Lady Vida about Katherine, but you can be sure the laird never will."

Tomas shook his head in disgust. It was just wrong.

"Tomas, lad, if you think anyone has forgotten Lady Katherine and the sacrifices she made for this clan, the fact that so many of us know who you are and haven't said anything should be testament to the contrary."

"I know and I understand. I just wish that Vida could know about her."

"Well, you've never vowed not to speak of Lady Katherine."

"I know, but I can't tell her without revealing who I am and I have no intention of doing that. I'm going home, in spite of what Laird Ruthven wants."

"What do you mean, *in spite of what he wants*?"

Tomas sighed. "This morning he called me into his solar to ask if I would stay on as his commander. It was all I could do not to laugh in his face."

Moyna's brows drew together. "Why would you laugh at that?"

"I can't be his commander. I can't work for him forever. After everything he's done? Nay, Moyna, I can't. Besides, I certainly couldn't live a lie for the rest of my life. I'm not Tomas MacHenry, one of Laird Carr's guardsmen."

"Well, let's consider this. What the laird did so many years ago was intended for his own selfish purposes, but as it turned out, it benefited others too. Lady Katherine is married to a man she loves, and who loves her back. That alone is miraculous. You are a fine man and a skilled warrior. Had you stayed here, if he didn't manage to kill you, you'd be working in the stables."

"That's because of Katherine, not him."

"But Katherine wouldn't have been able to help you if she hadn't been married to Laird MacIan. And as far as *working for him* goes, you're doing that now. Why did you agree to it?"

"Because I was worried about this clan. I still am. If someone decided to lay siege right now, I fear we wouldn't be able to defend Cotharach."

"So, you're working for *the clan*."

"Aye."

"Then if you stayed, wouldn't you still be working for the clan? Lady Katherine's clan? *Your* clan?"

"I have been a MacIan for nineteen years."

"I know. But let me ask you this, are you Laird MacIan's heir?"

"No, of course not. James is."

"Because…?"

"Because he's their natural son. It's the law."

"Aye, it's the law. Tomas, I know they love you because I know Lady Katherine. And maybe they would have wanted for you to have been their heir, but it can't be that way. Their oldest son will inherit his father's title and lands. And if something happened to him, the younger son would. And if something happened to him, their daughter and her husband would. And if something happened to her, you still might not be their heir if Laird MacIan has any blood relatives. Why? Because you were not born a MacIan. You were born a *Ruthven*. And the Ruthvens need you now more than the MacIans ever will."

She was right. Tomas knew she was, but he didn't want to accept it. "What about my identity? Like I said, I can't live a lie forever."

"Then don't. If you decide to stay, tell him who you are. Frankly, at this point, I don't think it will make a bit of difference. But if it does and he sends you packing, you've lost nothing. You intended to leave anyway."

"You have a point."

They sat in the silence of the church as Tomas thought through everything they'd discussed. Everything Moyna had said was true. Still, Tomas's heart was with his family in the Highlands. He was a MacIan and he was proud of it. But he couldn't deny, he was a Ruthven too, and that was why he was here in the first place.

He sighed. "I don't think I want to stay here forever. I love my family. But I can't deny that I'm needed here. What I will tell Laird Ruthven is that I will agree to be his commander in the short-term. I will stay as long as it takes to train, or hire someone to take my place."

"Will you tell him who you are?"

"I don't see the benefit in that. For now, I'll remain Tomas MacHenry."

"Well, that's fair enough for the time being. Now, come to the kitchen. I have nut-bread coming out of the oven and it was always your favorite."

He grinned, only too happy to comply.

Once back at the kitchen, Moyna gave him a loaf warm from the oven before he returned to the keep. He'd tell Ethan and Drew his plans first. Then, he'd find the laird.

He walked along, breaking off bits of the sweet bread and popping them in his mouth. As he stepped through the main doors, to his delight, Vida emerged from the stairs.

She smiled at him. "Good morning, Tomas."

He gave a slight bow. "Good morning. Ye're looking very beautiful this morn."

The comment had its desired effect. She looked down and blushed. By everything that was holy, he wanted to kiss her again. But before he could take a step towards her, he heard footsteps on the stairs. It was then that he noticed she carried a long mantle over one arm. "Where are you going on this fine day?"

"Moyna said she was baking sweet loaves this morning. So, I was planning to pay a few visits to some of our older clansmen and women and I'll take the loaves with me." She glanced at the half-eaten one in his hand and grinned. "That is if you've left any."

"Ah, lass, there were plenty to go around when I left the kitchen."

"Why were you in the kitchen anyway?"

He shrugged. "Why else? I love nut-bread and I heard she was baking this morning."

Vida laughed and said, "You're a rogue," just as her father stepped out of the stairwell.

"What's he done that makes him a rogue?" her father asked congenially.

"He beat me to the kitchens to get a sweet loaf before I delivered them all to the elders."

"Did he? I expect I'd better go as well if I want one for myself," her father teased.

"Oh, Papa, you know Moyna will set one aside for you. She always does. Now, if you'll both excuse me, I'll be on my way."

She took several steps towards the outer doors.

"Wait a moment," said Tomas. "Who'll be escorting ye?"

She laughed. "I don't need an escort. I'm just going to the village and it's broad daylight."

Tomas frowned. "My lady, I would prefer ye had an escort ere ye leave the castle walls."

She frowned. "I'm just going to the village. I don't need an escort. Tell him, Papa."

Laird Ruthven looked at Tomas. "You believe this is important?"

"Aye, sir, I do. She's precious to ye and she's just a lass. It may be overcautious, but better that than sorry."

"Papa, you've never sent a guard with me before. What could happen to me in the village?"

Her father frowned. "I don't want to find out. Nay, Tomas is right. Having a guardsman go with you is a reasonable precaution for your safety."

Vida scowled. "I have other things to do today. I don't have time to wait for you to arrange an escort."

Her father shrugged. "Well then, perhaps you should go with her today, Tomas. Vida won't be delayed and it will give you a chance to meet some of the clan elders."

"I'd be happy to, Laird."

The scowl on Vida's face shifted into a smile. "Well, if I won't be delayed…"

"Ye won't be," assured Tomas. "I'll just get my sword belt while ye go to the kitchen for the sweet loaves. I'll meet you there in a few moments."

"Very well, I'll meet ye there." She beamed at him before leaving the keep.

"Excuse me, Laird. I don't want to keep Lady Vida waiting."

He chuckled. "Nay, we wouldn't want that."

Much to his delight, Tomas spent the next hour or so visiting elders with Vida. He also realized that, like Moyna had said, many of these older people appeared to recognize him, presumably because of the resemblance he bore to his father. But also like Moyna, they didn't reveal that openly. Still, he could tell by the way they greeted him. And after chatting a few minutes with each of them, he couldn't deny that these people were important to him. He considered them his clansmen and women.

It wasn't until later that evening he was able to talk alone with Ethan and Drew and tell them about his decision.

"I'm not sure yer da's going to like this," said Drew.

"Not sure? I'm fairly certain he won't," said Ethan. "Staying here until spring is one thing. Staying longer? If the Ruthvens aren't yet prepared for a siege, that's madness."

"Then we will just have to work hard to see that they're ready," said Tomas.

101

"And if they're not? What of Lady Vida?" asked Ethan.

Tomas sighed heavily. "I'll send her to Duncurra with ye. She can come back when it's safe to do so."

"Her father will never agree to that," said Drew.

"I believe he will agree to anything I suggest, particularly where Vida's safety is concerned."

CHAPTER 10

August 3, 1378 (three months earlier)
On board the Mermaid Queen

Captain Daniel Lowther sat at the desk in his cabin to enter an account of the day into his private log. They were nearing the end of the last dogwatch. Although still twilight outside, it was too dark inside to see well enough to write. He chuckled to himself. There was a time in his youth when he might have been able to see the page but he hadn't been the captain of a vessel then. "Lord, why do ye waste such gifts on the young who have little need for them?"

He chuckled again. He had found himself asking the Almighty this same question too many times recently and always imagined the same answer: *My wisdom is not yours and this world is full of things you will never understand.*

He sighed, lit a lamp, opened his log, and dipped his quill in ink. After dating the entry he began to write:

> *We sailed from Cadiz on the morning high-tide, heading SSE along the Andalusian coast. A brisk northerly wind favored us for the first several hours and once at sea we averaged four knots. But an hour into the afternoon watch, the winds calmed, picking up only slightly about two hours later. Since that time we have averaged barely over a knot although now the wind appears to be shifting westerly and we are currently sailing at about two knots. Our current position is approximately ten knots due west of Cape*

Trafalgar. When we pass the headland, we will shift our course to the SE.

Of note is the fact that about two hours after leaving Cadiz, sails were spotted to the north. It is most likely another merchant vessel that left port after the Mermaid, but it has remained in our wake at too great a distance to identify it.

An urgent knock sounded at the door.

"Enter."

His cabin boy, Will, brow furrowed, entered the cabin, closing the door quickly behind him.

The captain frowned. "Lad, what has ye so concerned?"

"Captain, I think something's wrong."

The Captain had never seen Will appear so worried, even once when they'd sailed into the teeth of a fierce gale. "What is it?"

"That ship what's followed us all day, has begun to gain speed."

"The wind is picking up."

"Aye, sir, but she's been about ten knots back all day, now she's but five."

"Then the lookout should be able to see her colors."

"Aye, and he says she's a Portuguese merchant. Sir, she's still too far away for me to see much, but she doesn't look like any of the Portuguese ships that were in port nor do her colors resemble theirs. Plus, she seems high in the water—like she's empty. I asked the first mate if he'd let me look through the scope. He boxed my ears and told me to mind the hourglass."

Daniel frowned. Will was very bright and anxious to learn seafaring ways. Most of the men, including the first mate would usually spare a minute for him. "Was the sand running out, lad?" One of Will's primary responsibilities throughout the day was to turn the hourglass every half-hour to keep track of time. The men depended on this to know the start and end of each watch.

"Nay, sir. There were a few more minutes left. Some of the other hands seem to be behaving strangely too."

"How so?"

"Sort of nervous-like. Looking at the other ship. As soon as I turned the hourglass I slipped away down here. I thought you should know."

Daniel had had a variety of cabin boys over the years. Some skilled and dedicated, some less so. If nearly any one of those lads, even the best among them, brought him this tale, he'd have shrugged it off, crediting it to a lad's wild imagination. But Will was different. At only ten years old, he was what Daniel's dear, departed wife would have called an *old soul*. He was steady, and serious—never given to flights of fancy. If the lad was this worried, Daniel needed to take it seriously.

"Right, then, let's go topside and have a look." As he stood from his desk, a wave of foreboding passed through him. He'd learned years ago not to ignore feelings like that. "On second thought, lad, ready my cabin for me for the night. And stay here until I get back."

"But, Captain—"

"Don't argue with me, lad. If it is a Portuguese merchant, I'll come fetch you and give you a look. If it isn't, I don't want you on deck. Do you understand me?"

"Yes, sir."

Daniel left his cabin and climbed the stairs to the deck. The first mate was still at the helm.

"Good evening, Captain."

"Good evening, Desmond. Any report for me?"

"Nay, Captain. All's quiet."

Daniel looked around, assessing the wind and the *Mermaid*'s speed. They'd slowed down again, but the sails weren't set to make the best use of the light wind they had. "Where is the Sailing Master?"

"He's below, having his supper."

"Did you not pay attention to the shifting winds? The sails need adjusting."

"The winds have just now turned, Captain. I was preparing to get right on that."

The Captain looked aft, and indeed, as Will had said, the other ship was gaining on them at an alarming speed. Irritated, he asked, "And the ship in our wake isn't worthy of report?"

"No, sir," answered the Mate. "It's just a Portuguese merchant."

"Give me the scope."

"Certainly, Captain."

The Mate handed him the telescope. Daniel lifted it to his eye. In the growing gloom it wasn't easy to see. He moved toward the aft rail, adjusting the focus. "That isn't a Portuguese Merchant…" something struck him in the back of the head. For an instant, all he felt was blinding pain, then nothing.

CHAPTER 11

Ambrose thought things were finally going his way. Four weeks ago, after the first message from Lindsay arrived, he had asked Tomas MacHenry to stay on permanently. The lad hadn't agreed outright, but said he would stay until there was someone to replace him.

Gregor hadn't been the least bit put out by this. He agreed that convincing Tomas to stay was in everyone's best interest, including his own. Looking back over the last two months, Gregor said he could scarcely believe how much his own skills had improved. He wasn't anxious for the Carrs to leave.

The clan seemed to love the Carr warriors in general and Tomas specifically. Ambrose simply had to find a way to persuade him to stay.

But tonight, an unwelcome message had arrived during the evening meal. Ambrose took one look at the seal and slipped it into the sleeve of his tunic.

Unfortunately, this messenger hadn't arrived during a feast, and Vida took notice.

"Who is the message from, Papa?"

"It's nothing important, my darling."

She frowned. "But who is it from?"

"It's from Naughton Lindsay. You know, he's an old friend of mine."

"Does it have something to do with the ship that hasn't returned? He invests in imports and exports too, does he not?"

"Aye, he does, but it's not about that."

"How do you know? You didn't open it."

"I know, because I know. And I didn't open it because I don't have to. I'll open it later. Now let this drop, Davida."

She frowned and looked hurt, but said no more.

Ambrose hated distressing her so, but the truth would be worse. He had to think about his options. "Excuse me. I've had enough supper. I'm going to retire for the evening." As he stood to leave the table, it occurred to him he needed to discuss this with someone who had a general knowledge of the law. "Father Michael, I would appreciate a few minutes of your time when you've finished dining. I'll be in my solar."

"Certainly, Laird. I can come now if you wish."

"Nay, that isn't necessary. There's no rush. Enjoy your supper first."

"As you wish, Laird."

Ambrose left the table, but felt the stares of everyone in the hall as he left. Once in the privacy of his solar, he opened the missive. Much to his dismay, this one was not from Naughton. It was from his brother, Laird Lindsay.

Ambrose, by the grace of God, Laird Ruthven,

It has come to my attention that my younger brother, Naughton, entered into an agreement with you concerning a debt you incurred August last. Please be assured that a debt to Naughton is a debt to me.

I understand said debt was guaranteed with funds to be gained from the sale of a shipment of Genoese goods, which is now long overdue. Alternatively, my brother agreed to accept your daughter's hand in marriage and the debt would be forgiven.

I fear you must accept that the Mermaid Queen has been lost, as several vessels leaving port after yours have long since returned. I understand payment on the debt is due by the end of December. If we have not received the full amount by then, I will arrive at your gates on Hogmanay. You will either pay your debt then, sign the betrothal between Davida and my brother, or I will take what is owed me.

Sincerely,

Howard, Laird Lindsay

There had been no word from anyone about his ship. Laird Lindsay was right, several other ships had returned over the last few weeks. The news from those captains didn't bode well. No one had seen the *Mermaid Queen* since it left Cadiz, where it had stopped to take on provisions. It never arrived in Genoa.

The idea that he promised Vida's hand as a guarantee was preposterous. He would pay Lindsay back. True, he couldn't pay absolutely all of it immediately or he wouldn't have sufficient money to ensure the clan's survival through the winter months. But the *Merry Mistress* might return as early as January, and certainly by March. Surely, it wasn't lost too. No one has that much bad luck. The reason he invested in a second Mediterranean-bound ship was to mitigate losses should something happen to one of them. And even if the worst happened, he still had his other ships that had sailed to the Baltics in October, after the fall harvest was in. They too might be back as early as January if the weather didn't turn foul.

Aye, he had ways of paying the debt eventually. Were the issue of a betrothal to Vida not in the mix, this wouldn't present a problem. Naughton would have to accept the bulk of what Ambrose owed him and renegotiate the remainder of the debt.

But what Ambrose thought had been a jest, Naughton was taking seriously, and now he had the might of Clan Lindsay behind him. Unless Ambrose could prove to Laird Lindsay that it had only been a jest, and Ambrose doubted that was possible, Lindsay could have an army at his gates on the first of January. Then Ambrose would only have two options, pay what he owed and risk the safety of his clan, or fight…and risk the safety of his clan. Because, as long as he drew breath, he would not marry Vida to Naughton Lindsay.

His thoughts were interrupted by a knock at the door. "Enter."

Father Michael stepped into the room. He was a tall, slender man with sandy hair who was not much younger than Ambrose himself. But unlike Ambrose, he had been educated in a university as priests from affluent families often were. He would know enough about the laws to help sort this mess out. "You wished to see me, Laird?"

"Aye, Father." Ambrose motioned towards a chair. "Please, make yourself comfortable."

Father Michael sat in the chair opposite Ambrose and steepled his forefingers under his chin, as was his habit when he was listening.

Ambrose proceeded to tell him everything.

When he had finished, Father Michael appeared to consider things before asking, "Was anyone else present when you entered into the financial arrangement?"

"Aye, several men. A couple of Laird Ogilvie's sons were there, as was Laird Gow's heir. Laird Rattray and Laird MacNab were there too."

"Are any of these men close allies of yours?"

Ambrose frowned. He hadn't really expended much effort in building close ties over the years. "None of them are enemies…except for Gow, I suppose. And that's only since he started raiding my land. I've done nothing to provoke him. Why does it matter if they are allies?"

"Because, Laird, I fear Naughton's statement that you considered a jest, could be construed as a verbal contract."

"How is that possible? I never agreed to it."

"Tell me again exactly what was said."

"We were in the midst of a game of chance. I had lost a considerable sum, but I had the chance to recoup my losses. I asked if anyone would extend me credit. Naughton asked what guarantee I could offer that the debt would be repaid. I told him I had two ships heading to Mediterranean ports, each of which would bring at least four times what I would owe him, including interest. He agreed that the payoff from Mediterranean ships was enormous. Then he said, 'I'm sure you're good for it. And never fear, if something goes awry, you can give me your daughter's hand in marriage instead.' I laughed, but I didn't agree to that."

"But you didn't disagree? You didn't tell him you wouldn't bargain with your daughter's hand?"

"Well, no. Everyone laughed. It was just a jest. At the time, I didn't want to insult anyone by taking it seriously. And I believed I couldn't lose."

Father Michael arched an eyebrow but didn't comment. "Was anything else said about it?"

Ambrose thought for a moment. "We negotiated the terms. We agreed on the amount of interest that would be paid and that the debt would come due when the *Mermaid Queen* returned to Dundee, or the end of December, whichever came first."

"So, you captured the agreement in writing."

"Nay, we were in the middle of a game."

"So, you finished the game and you lost. Did you write the agreement down then?"

Ambrose was becoming exasperated. What was so hard to understand? "Nay, Father. It was an agreement between gentlemen, witnessed by others, it didn't need to be written. When the game was over, I left the table."

"And he said no more?"

"Nay, he laughed and said he'd see me in December if not before, but that marriage to Vida would be well worth his investment too. Everyone laughed again."

"And you didn't clarify at that point?"

"Father, it was a joke."

"Laird, I'm sorry, but I fear it wasn't. You have no written agreement. In the context of agreeing to the loan, Lindsay included two ways to repay him and you didn't clarify that. He implied that Vida's hand was the price of defaulting on the loan as you left and you still didn't clarify."

"But there were witnesses. Any reasonable man would have seen it as a jest and not part of the agreement."

"Any reasonable man who was a friend of yours might see it that way. But I fear you didn't have friends at the table. Laird Lindsay and Laird Ogilvie are extremely close allies. Rattray and Ogilvie are as well. I'm not certain if Gow has any formal relationship with any of the others, but he certainly doesn't have a good relationship with you. MacNab might be the only one who would see things differently, but one lone voice wouldn't be enough."

"Oh, dear God. I didn't mean…I never would have…Father, I swear I didn't think he was serious."

"Do you have enough funds to pay the debt?"

"Almost. I could pay ninety percent and have absolutely nothing left. If he'd accept eighty percent, we'd have enough left to manage until the *Merry Mistress*, or one of my other ships, return. I can renegotiate the small debt that remains and agree to pay more interest on it."

Father Michael shook his head. "Laird, ye're missing the point. The only reason Lindsay would have to renegotiate the terms of the contract would be if you couldn't make good on it."

"I can't make good on it."

"Sadly, Laird, you can. If Vida is unwed by Hogmanay, and you can't pay your debt *in full*, he has every legal right to claim her hand."

Ambrose couldn't believe what he was hearing. "How could that off-handed comment have become part of the agreement? I never meant that. I'd never have agreed to it."

"Laird, the Lord Sheriff in Perth could be called upon to adjudicate, but I don't believe he would find in your favor."

Ambrose put his head in his hands, and moaned, "What am I going to do? I cannot agree to the betrothal."

"Do you have an ally who would loan you the money to cover the debt?"

Did he? He wracked his brain, trying to think of someone who might extend him a small amount of credit, but came up with nothing.

Father shrugged. "Then I only see one option and there is a risk involved."

"What is it? I'll do anything."

"If Vida is married before Hogmanay, she cannot be given to someone else. Then, if you could not repay the full debt, Lindsay would be forced to renegotiate, or you would go to debtors' prison until the loan was fully repaid."

"Debtors' prison is a risk I would take."

"I assumed you would, but that's not the risk I meant."

"What else could happen?"

"For a moment let's just assume that you can find a suitable husband for her. I believe you when you say you did not intend to enter into a betrothal agreement and nothing exists in writing which disputes that. So, I can agree to conduct the wedding. However, I will have to post the banns for three Sundays beforehand. It's possible that word of the pending wedding could reach Lindsay. That is, after all, why the Church requires the banns—so any impediments to marriage might be identified. Then, he could challenge

Vida's freedom to marry because of the verbal agreement for a betrothal he believes he has."

"What could happen then?"

"Again, he'd have to take ye before the Lord Sheriff. If the sheriff agreed you were trying to default on the loan by marrying Vida to someone else, he could block the wedding and force the loan to be paid immediately. Then if you couldn't pay the full amount, Vida would be forced to marry Naughton and no one could stop it."

Ambrose sat considering the awful consequences of what he had done. There had to be a way out of this. Then an idea formed. "What if I sent her away? What if I had the Carrs escort her to the Highlands?"

"Laird, you don't seem to understand. Even if Vida is not here when Laird Lindsay arrives on Hogmanay, if you can't pay the debt, a betrothal exists. Vida cannot marry anyone else as long as it does. If Lindsay ever found her, even years from now, her first marriage will be nullified. Any children from that marriage would be bastards. She would be forced to marry Lindsay and he would ultimately become Laird of Clan Ruthven."

"There are no other options?" Ambrose heard the desperation in his voice.

Father Michael sighed. "She could take religious vows."

"Send her to a convent?" Ambrose brightened. "Well, that's the answer. She can go to a convent until I can pay back everything I owe. It will only be a few months at most."

Father Michael shook his head, clearly frustrated. "Laird, I don't know how many different ways I can tell you this. If you do not pay the full amount owed to Lindsay by the last day of December, a betrothal exists. It doesn't matter if you can pay ninety-nine percent of what you owe. It doesn't matter if you only lack a farthing. It doesn't even matter if you can pay him double the entire debt on the first of January. He is not required to accept anything less than payment in full by the end of December. Failing this, he can exercise his right to a betrothal in lieu of payment."

"But if she's in a convent, if he wants his money back, he'll have to accept it, and once he does, there will be no betrothal."

"That's true, but he has no reason to accept it. He's a bright man and, clearly, he has his sights set on Clan Ruthven. He would have to assume entering the convent was a ploy. He need only sit and wait. If Vida leaves the convent, she is his. If she doesn't, it is highly likely the leadership of Clan Ruthven would be given to him on your death anyway."

"Simply because he was betrothed to Vida?"

"Aye, a case could be made. So, you can see how being your heir is ultimately much more valuable than the gold you owe him."

Ambrose put his head in his hands. "I've failed her. What do I do?"

"Tell her and let her choose."

"I can't do that!"

Father shrugged. "Well then, there is only one choice that assures she will not have to marry Naughton and that is for her to enter a convent for what is likely to be the rest of her life."

"Send her away forever? I can't do that either."

Father shook his head. "This is why you should leave the choice to her. But if you refuse to do that, the next best chance is to see her married as soon as possible and pray Lindsay doesn't hear about it until after the wedding."

Ambrose nodded resolutely. "Aye. That's what we'll have to do."

"You must realize that may be easier said than done. You will need to identify a worthy groom before the twelfth day of December at the latest, to give us three Sundays and still be able to have the wedding before the last day of the month. The third Sunday would be St. Stephen's Day, so we could have the wedding the next day, on the feast of Saint John."

"That's cutting things awfully close. What if we posted the banns this Sunday? The wedding could be a week earlier."

"Nay, it couldn't. I can't perform a marriage during Advent, so the earliest possible day for the wedding would only be two days earlier on Christmas."

"Aye, well then, the twelfth it is. Now, it's just a matter of finding a groom."

"Laird, that's no small matter, but allow me to make a suggestion."

"Of course. At this point I'll consider anything."

"Would you consider asking Sir Tomas?"

Ambrose frowned. "Sir Tomas?"

"Aye. He's a good man and an excellent leader. Clearly, you think so yourself, because you want him to stay as your commander."

"Aye, I can't dispute that."

"Not to mention the fact that Vida is clearly fond of him and I suspect he harbors warm feelings for her as well."

Ambrose cocked his head. "Really?"

"Aye."

Ambrose frowned. "But he isn't a nobleman."

"Are you certain?"

"I…I guess I don't really know. I just assumed so. He hasn't claimed to be a nobleman."

"He could be the younger son of a younger son. Actually, I suspect all three of them are of noble houses. They all read and have the manners I would expect of noblemen."

Ambrose frowned. "Those things are true. I hadn't thought of that possibility. But why would they be part of Laird Carr's guard then?"

"Highlanders do that. If they have sons living and working among other clans, their alliances are stronger."

"Then I'll ask Tomas if he's a nobleman."

The priest shook his head. "I don't advise that."

"Why not?"

"Laird, you really only have one choice. You have not opened negotiations with anyone else, and if you begin asking now, you have no hope of keeping your plan secret. Besides, anyone in his right mind would have to wonder why the rush now and would be hesitant to agree. If your search for a husband leaves these walls, you can be certain it will get back to Lindsay. Perhaps even before the first banns are posted."

"But if Tomas isn't a nobleman, maybe one of the other two are?"

"Laird, forgive me, but you are losing sight of your daughter in all of this. She likes Sir Tomas. I'm certain she would not be opposed to such a union, especially if she understands the reasons for it. She is the one who must now bear the brunt of the consequences for your actions. It would seem to me ensuring she has at least a hope for happiness would be paramount."

Ambrose sighed. "You're right. Of course, you are."

"So, would you like for me to inform Sir Tomas that you wish to speak to him?"

"Aye, there's no time like the present."

CHAPTER 12

Tomas had just lost another chess game to Vida. Every time he played with her, he knew the instant she was certain of winning. She grew quiet, frowned slightly, her cheeks went pink, and she chewed on her bottom lip. It would have been entirely adorable except that he knew this was her response because she was somehow ashamed of beating him. If he stayed here very long, he'd have to figure out a way to stop this.

"Would you like to play again, Tomas?" she asked hesitantly. It was as if she feared someday he would say no.

"One more game tonight, then I need to get some rest."

Her face lit with a happy smile and she began to set up the board. Oh, the things that smile did to him.

So distracted was he that he didn't notice Father Michael approaching them until the priest spoke. "Lady Vida, Sir Tomas, please pardon the interruption."

"Good evening, Father," said Tomas. "Would ye care to join us? Perhaps the two of us together could manage a victory."

Father laughed. "Don't count on it."

"Perhaps the two of you would like to play and I'll watch," said Vida.

Father Michael smiled. "While I'm certain I'd enjoy that, your father has asked to speak with Sir Tomas. Shall I take his place?"

Tomas had no idea what the laird wanted with him, but he was fairly certain it must have something to do with the missive he received.

A frown flitted briefly across Vida's face, but she replied, "Of course, Father. It's been a while since we've had a game."

Tomas stood up. "Thank ye, Father. Please excuse me, Lady Vida."

Father Michael took Tomas's seat. "You'll find the laird in his solar. He's expecting you."

Tomas nodded. "Aye. Thank ye."

He made his way to the solar and knocked on the door.

The laird called, "Enter."

Tomas stepped in the room and closed the door behind him. Laird Ruthven paced in front of the hearth, obviously upset by something.

"Father Michael said you wished to speak with me."

"Aye. Sit down. We need to talk."

Tomas frowned and sat in one of the chairs by the hearth. This was a glimpse of the Ambrose Ruthven Tomas remembered.

Ruthven took the chair opposite him. "I have to tell you something. I'm not proud of it, but I can't change it now and we have to deal with it."

Over the next three quarters of an hour, Tomas listened to a sordid tale that began with Ruthven overextending himself in a game of chance. It moved on to a missing ship, a shortfall of funds, and a misunderstanding that meant Vida would have to marry her father's creditor if the entire debt couldn't be paid by the last day of December.

Ambrose ended by saying, "I don't have quite enough money to pay the debt and can't let her marry that man. Father Michael believes it wasn't what I intended, but he's equally certain that if forced to go before the sheriff, the sheriff will rule that a verbal contract existed."

Tomas wanted to rail at the man for being an idiot. How could he even have joked about Vida's hand in marriage? How could he incur such a debt in a foolish game of chance in the first place? But all that was water under the bridge now. "Why does Father think that?"

"Because all but one of the other men there were friends or allies of Lindsay."

"Who else was there?"

"Two of Laird Ogilvie's sons. Ogilvie and Lindsay are close allies. Laird MacNab and Laird Rattray were there. Rattray is a close ally of Ogilvie. And Gow's heir was there too."

"A Gow was there? And you didn't think it was important to tell me all of this when we learned Gow was one of the people raiding yer land?"

"You think they're connected?"

Tomas stared at him. How had the Ruthvens managed to survive the last nineteen years under his leadership? "Aye, sir, I think they're connected. Every man at that table knows you were way overextended. It's likely not a coincidence that nearly every man there was connected to the Lindsay's in some way. For that matter, I suspect MacNab is too, we just don't know how yet. Tell me, before that night, had Naughton Lindsay ever mentioned a betrothal?"

Ruthven frowned. "Aye. Many times. I'd always turned him down. That's why I thought it was a jest. He knew I'd never agree to a betrothal between him and Vida."

"By all that's good and holy," swore Tomas. "Laird, ye were set up. I wouldn't be surprised if they somehow managed to rig the game so ye'd lose, but there's no way to prove that. I am absolutely certain Lindsay entered into that game intending to come out of it with ye in his debt and at least the potential to win Vida's hand."

"Maybe so, but if my ship had returned from Genoa, it wouldn't have mattered. He can't have had anything to do with that."

"It doesn't seem possible, but I'm not certain of anything at the moment. Is there any way at all out of this mess? Do ye have enough to pay the debt?"

"Almost."

"So, that would be nay, ye don't."

Ambrose winced. "I had planned to pay the largest portion of it and renegotiate what remained."

"There is no way he'll do that. The money was never the issue. He ultimately wants to marry Vida so he can be Laird of Clan Ruthven." *God's bloody bones.* Fate couldn't deal a more appropriate blow to the current man who'd weaseled his way into that title, than having it taken in the exact same way. But just like before, the person who stood to lose the most was an innocent.

"Aye, that's what Father Michael said. All along I thought it was simply about the money."

Tomas shook his head. "Did Father have any other suggestions?"

"He said, because there isn't a written agreement, Vida could marry someone else before the end of December. He said the banns would have to be posted and there would be no guarantee Lindsay wouldn't challenge the legality of it before the wedding. But if he didn't, the marriage would be valid."

"And if he challenges it?"

"The Lord Sheriff in Perth would hear the case and most likely rule in Lindsay's favor. I'd have to pay the debt in full, or Vida would have to marry Naughton."

"*Christ almighty*, man, how did ye let this happen?"

Ambrose just shook his head. He looked old and beaten.

The time had arrived. Tomas could deal the death blow by simply leaving. He could maybe even convince Vida to run away with him. But Moyna and Katherine came to his mind. It wasn't the action they would take and neither of them would ever respect him again if he did.

"How much can ye afford to pay him?"

"If I give him every last farthing, I can cover about ninety percent of the debt, but I'd have nothing left for the clan and winter is coming. If I only had to pay eighty percent of it, with economies, I think the clan could get along until one of my other ships arrives. If I can manage to have her married without Lindsay finding out, he'll have no choice but to negotiate."

"Or throw ye into debtors' prison until the loan is paid off." It nearly killed Tomas to ask this next question. "Do ye have an appropriate husband for her in mind?"

"I do. At least, I know the man who I'd like for her to marry. Obviously, I haven't approached him yet."

"Then see it done. Your clan's financial affairs are none of my business." Tomas stood and started walking toward the door.

"Sir Tomas, you're the man I'd like for her to marry."

Had he heard that correctly? Tomas turned back around. "Excuse me?"

"You have every skill needed to lead this clan. Skills that I confess, I've never had. You will make a fine laird someday and I have reason to believe she's fond of you."

By all that was holy, Tomas was more than fond of her, but that didn't change who her father was. "I can't marry yer daughter. Ye don't know who I am."

"Please, don't say no without thinking about it. Think about what you'll gain. You will be a nobleman, eventually the laird of this clan. If managed well, Cotharach can be profitable. It was when my brother was in charge of it. You are a good man. You would be a gentle husband for my daughter. I can want nothing more for her."

"You want *me* to marry your daughter and become Laird Ruthven?"

"Yes."

"Ye're absolutely certain about that?"

"Yes. Please, Sir Tomas. You are my only hope."

Tomas gave a mirthless chuckle. "Well, Laird Ruthven, this is a surprise."

Tomas could marry her, then as her husband, take her with him to the Highlands. There would be nothing Ruthven could do. "I'll think about it."

CHAPTER 13

Tomas's head was spinning. He could hardly believe tonight's turn of events and he needed to discuss it with Drew and Ethan. It was late and he assumed they'd gone to bed, but this couldn't wait.

He first knocked on Ethan's door.

Ethan answered it within seconds, pulling his clothes on, his sword belt in hand. "What's happened?"

"Nothing. I mean nothing that ye need yer weapons for, but something has happened that I need to discuss with ye and Drew immediately."

"Give me just a minute. I'll finish dressing."

Then Tomas knocked on Drew's door and was met with a response so similar to that of Ethan's he couldn't help laughing.

"Finish dressing, put yer weapons away, and come to my chamber. We need to talk."

By the time he had candles lit, they were both present. "Sit down. This will take a while."

He told them the story Ruthven had. Only he was able to interject his personal opinions of how colossally stupid Ambrose had been. When he told them about Ruthven's desire for him to marry Vida, both men broke into spasms of laughter.

Ethan was the first one to regain enough control to speak. "God's teeth, Tomas, this is the most perfect possible revenge. The stable hand who was his whipping boy has now become his savior and will be the Laird of this clan."

Tomas shook his head. "Part of me wants to finish him completely and take the heart of his heart to Duncurra."

"Ye can't do that," admonished Drew.

"I know," said Tomas. "Taking Vida away from her father and her people would be every bit as bad as it was for Ambrose to send Lady Katherine away."

"What are ye going to do then?" asked Drew.

"I've been thinking. The amount Ruthven owes Lindsay is huge, but he has most of it. The problem with simply marrying Vida is that if Lindsay catches wind of it, he could block it legally and if Ambrose can't pay the full amount, the sheriff could force Vida to marry Lindsay."

"Then we have to figure out a way to get the money before that happens," said Ethan.

"Aye, that is exactly what I was thinking."

"I'm sure Laird MacLennan would help," said Drew.

"I expect he would. Between him and my parents, it shouldn't pose a problem. But I need to send a message to them immediately so they can have time to gather it and get here."

A grin split Ethan's face. "Besides, yer mother would be furious if she weren't here for yer wedding."

Tomas frowned. "About that…"

"What about it?" Asked Drew. "Don't deny that ye adore Vida. And now her papa has practically begged ye to marry her."

Tomas nodded. "I know. And I would love to marry her. But not like this. Not as my mother had to do."

"I thought there was no other option," said Ethan.

"There wouldn't be, if her father couldn't pay the full debt. But we know, with a little help from the MacIans and the MacLennans, he can. If she marries me, I want it to be her choice. I'm going to talk to her first thing in the morning and tell her everything."

Drew frowned. "It will kill her to find out what her father's done."

Ethan nodded. "He's right, it will. Maybe it's better to try to spare her a little of the pain."

He understood why his friends thought that, and their hearts were in the right place, but they were wrong. "I know it might hurt her. In fact, it most assuredly *will* hurt her. But I've gotten to know Vida over the last few weeks. She is extraordinarily smart. I have yet to win a game of chess."

"Ye're jesting," said Ethan. "I can almost never beat ye."

"I can't either," said Drew.

"So ye understand what I mean. But the first night we played, she was three moves from checkmate and she threw the game. I made her go back and make the correct move. Even now, she seems unsure and embarrassed every time she wins. She is probably the only reason Cotharach has remained afloat for the last few years—even Ambrose admits that. But she always acts in her father's name and gives him the credit. For the love of all that's holy, *she* was the one who felt guilty that the men-at-arms lacked skills."

"How could she be responsible for that?" asked Drew.

"Because she has spent most of her life *managing* her father. Helping him control his anger, not to mention his bouts of stupidity, while not injuring his pride. Learning all of this is going to shatter her. But she deserves to know so that she can be the one to consider all of the options and then make the choice for herself. If it is her choice, I would like nothing more than to marry her. But if it isn't, she doesn't need to be forced. We can give her another option."

Both of his friends agreed. It was for the best.

"So, I need the two of ye to get home as soon as ye can."

"Both of us don't need to go," said Drew. "Ethan can deliver the message to Laird MacLennan on his way to Duncurra."

Tomas shook his head. "Nay. One of ye traveling alone is too much of a risk. It's possible Lindsay has men watching to stop anything Ambrose might have planned. I doubt it. I suspect he thinks Ambrose is too stupid to find a way out, but we can't risk it. In fact, once ye reach Laird Carr, I'd prefer if he'd allow several men to go the rest of the way with ye."

"Very well," said Drew. "We'll leave at first light. With any luck, we'll be back with a few coins and yer parents before Christmas. But ye know, it will give away yer identity."

"I know. I'm going to tell Vida anyway. We'll figure out what to tell her father."

Ethan clasped his hands together in supplication. "Oh please, please, don't tell him until we get back. I want to see the look on his face when he realizes who is actually saving his arse."

Tomas chuckled. "We'll see."

~ * ~

Tomas was up before first light to bid farewell to his friends. He'd figure out something to tell Laird Ruthven about their sudden departure. Then he went to the great hall. If the day went as it usually did, Vida would be up soon, well before her father. Tomas would take her to the chapel, so they could have privacy.

He didn't have to wait long.

She entered the hall and her face lit with a smile when she saw him. "Good morning, Tomas. You didn't come back last night."

"I'm sorry. I would have liked to, but yer father and I had a great deal to discuss. It was late when we finished."

Her brows drew together. "That sounds serious."

"We did talk about some serious matters and I would like to discuss them with ye."

"Why didn't Papa just ask me to come too? He could have told us both at the same time."

"Aye that would have been nice, but to be perfectly honest, there are some things he doesn't wish ye to know. However, I think you must be informed. Ye are truly the one who runs this clan, not him."

"Nay, ye're wrong. He's Laird Ruthven."

"I know." He gave her a sad smile. "And ye just threw a chess game."

She tilted her head to one side. A look of confusion on her face. "I don't understand."

"Vida, ye have done a very good job of making yer father, and maybe a few other people, believe he runs this clan. But most everyone here knows the truth. Like me, they notice when ye *throw the chess game*, when ye do something that allows him to get the credit."

She blushed and shook her head. "You misunderstand…"

"Nay, I don't. Come with me now, please. This is extremely important. I'd let ye break yer fast first, but I must talk to ye before yer father comes down for the day." He held a hand out to her.

"Where are we going?" She took his hand.

"To the chapel. It's the most private place I know of for this conversation. But first ye need to go get a mantle."

"If ye really want to avoid my papa, I can't. I heard him moving around his chamber as I was leaving mine. He might be down any minute."

Tomas smiled at the thought of holding her close to keep her warm, but this was going to take a while and the chapel would be cold. "I'll fetch something to keep ye warm then. If ye hear yer da coming, hide."

She smiled and nodded, her eyes sparkling, perhaps at the idea of a wee bit of mischief. Was it possible that this remarkable woman could possibly become his?

He ran up to his room, grabbed an extra plaid, and was back down in moments. He wrapped it around her, covering her head against the frosty morning wind. Seeing her wrapped in his plaid caused the heat to stir in his belly. This was what he wanted, to care for her, love her, and keep her safe forever.

Once they were in the chapel. He asked her to sit with him on a bench. "What I'm about to tell ye will be hard to hear. I can't tell ye the truth and make it any easier. It is vitally important and will influence the rest of yer life. I promise ye. But if ye don't want to hear it, I'll respect that."

"Ye're scaring me."

"I'm sorry, but I need to know, do ye want me to go on?"

"Aye, of course I do."

"Very well." He took her hands in his and told her everything he'd learned up to the moment he left her father's solar last night.

When he'd finished, tears stood in her eyes. "You shouldn't have to marry me to fix my father's mess."

He gathered her in his arms. "Oh nay, lass, I want nothing more than to marry ye." He cupped her face in his hand and kissed her tenderly. When he pulled away, she looked so very young and fragile, it caused his heart to ache. "Of course, I want to marry ye. Never doubt that. And if it is yer choice to, I'll be a very happy man. But I didn't think it was right to force ye into this. Ye're one of the smartest people I've ever known. Not telling ye everything, not letting ye consider all of the consequences and make this decision yerself, would be wrong, regardless of what I want."

"I do want to marry ye, Tomas. But I'm afraid. What if Naughton Lindsay does learn of it? Papa can't pay, and I'd be forced to marry him."

"My precious lass, put yer mind at ease. I can get the remaining money."

"How?"

"That is another story that I'm afraid isn't going to be easy to hear. But if ye wish to marry me, ye must know."

She nodded. "I'm not sure it can be any worse."

Tomas sighed. "I fear it is. Do ye remember when ye told me yer uncle Ainsley died with no children?"

"Aye. My papa wouldn't be laird otherwise."

"Well, that isn't quite true. Yer uncle had a daughter. Her name is Katherine."

Vida frowned. "Her name *is* Katherine. She's still alive."

Tomas laughed. "She's very much alive." He told her the story of Ambrose trading Katherine's title and lands for a larger dowry in coin."

Vida's hands flew to her mouth, a look of utter shock on her face. "Oh, dear God…my father did essentially what Naughton Lindsay is doing. He *bought* the title of Laird Ruthven using a forced marriage."

"Aye. I'm afraid so, although I'm not sure *he* sees it that way."

"Tomas, this is awful. How is that you know this and for the love of God, why did no one ever tell me?"

"According to Moyna, no one ever told ye because yer father forbade it. And the reason why I know about it in the first place is because I was here when it happened."

"How could you have been here?"

"I was a member of this clan. I was born here. My parents died when I was very young. I lived with my grandfather who was the stable master. When I was old enough, I worked as a stable boy. My grandfather died just before I turned seven." He saved her from the worst part of the story, the details of her father's cruelty. "I had no one, so when Lady Katherine left, she took me with them."

"But ye're a Carr. Did they leave ye with Laird Carr?"

He smiled. "Nay, I'm a MacIan. They adopted me." He told her why he was with Laird Carr and why they decided not to let her father know the truth.

"So, you're a MacIan. You're my cousin's son."

"Her adopted son, but aye, I'm a MacIan. I sent Ethan and Drew to the Highlands this morning with a message for my parents. I'm certain they'll bring the funds needed to completely pay off the debt."

"But why would Katherine do that, after what my father did to her? Why would she help us?"

He smiled broadly and kissed her temple. "Tell me, my sweet lass, if the situation were reversed, if ye were Katherine and she were ye, what would ye do?"

She smiled. "I'd bring the gold."

"Why?"

"Because I love my clan and in the grand scheme of things, it is for them."

"And that is exactly why my mother will. She loves this clan. It is also why I stayed. I was raised as a MacIan, but these are my people too. And if ye're still willing to marry me after learning I was the stable boy here before ye were born, I swear to ye, I will always consider the needs of the clan above all else."

"Of course, I want to marry ye. Tomas, I love ye. No one has ever treated me like ye do."

"Even though I just shattered a number of illusions for ye?"

She chuckled. "Partly *because* ye did that. Ye valued me and my opinions and feelings enough to tell me the truth."

"I love ye too, Vida. I tried not to because I didn't think ye could ever be mine, but I couldn't do it. I love ye with everything in me." He leaned down and captured her lips in a kiss. She opened her mouth to him, warm and inviting. He deepened the kiss and became lost in her. A noise finally penetrated his brain and he ended the kiss.

The noise was Father Michael clearing his throat.

"Uh...Father...good morning."

Embarrassed, Vida tucked her face against Tomas's chest, looking as if she wanted to disappear.

The priest smiled. "Aye, it looks as if it's a very good morning."

"We just came here for a bit of privacy."

"I see." He looked completely amused.

"I mean, there were some things I needed to talk to Lady Vida about."

The priest nodded. "Excellent. I was hoping you'd have the sense to do that. Do you need a little more time…to talk?"

"Just a minute, if you don't mind," said Vida, surprising both men.

"Not at all, my Lady. I'll take a short walk and be right back." He left the chapel.

"Vida, my love, I think I've told ye everything I know."

"Aye, but there is something I think we still need to consider."

"What's that?"

"If my father finds out who you really are, that the MacIan's adopted you and that they are on their way here with enough coin to help pay off the debt, he might change his mind about allowing us to marry."

"I hadn't thought about that."

She smiled. "I know how my papa's mind works…at least most of the time. Let's allow him to act on what he believes to be true. At least for a while."

"Vida, he's bound to know something's up when my parents ride through the gates."

She laughed, the sound fanning the flame of desire that had begun to burn in his belly.

"Let's worry about that when it happens. I think it is better to keep Papa in the dark until the funds actually arrive."

"As you wish, my lady."

He kissed her again, only letting her go when one more time they were interrupted by Father Michael.

"I thought ye were going to talk," he said in mock exasperation.

"I'm sorry, Father. But how can ye blame me. I have a beautiful woman in my arms. I'd be an embarrassment to Highlanders if I didn't kiss her."

CHAPTER 14

It was still early when Vida returned to the great hall, but she felt as if it had been hours—even days—not minutes since she had left. Tomas did not enter the hall with her. She didn't want to have to explain anything. She let go of his hand, gave him a quick kiss, and returned his plaid just before running up the steps and through the front doors. She was sharply aware of the instant loss of warmth, both from his heavy wool wrap and his mere presence. Still, she smiled and hugged herself. It wouldn't be long before they were married. Today was the first day of December, so she only had to wait twenty-six days.

When she reached the table, she poured herself a goblet of watered wine and sat down to nibble on a bannock and think. The things she had heard about her father distressed her. He had left the running of the clan largely to her. If he had told her about the debt as soon as it had been incurred, she could have taken steps to reduce spending then. She might have been able to ensure they had enough to live on, just in case something happened.

But her father hadn't been able to imagine that anything would go wrong. That was one of his biggest faults. Although he might occasionally consider her too, he rarely looked beyond his needs in the moment. He didn't want her to know what he'd done and he didn't believe she'd ever need to, so he kept on spending as if he had no financial worries.

Until the ship actually came in bearing a profitable cargo, Vida would have assumed it might not. She didn't expect the worst, but she certainly believed in planning for it.

The fact that her father had allowed Naughton Lindsay to think he would insure the debt with a betrothal left her dumbfounded. But again, she knew why her father had done it, even if he didn't know it himself. She was fairly certain he believed that if he had treated the comment as anything more than a jest, Lindsay wouldn't have loaned him the money. But because he was unable to look ahead and accept the possibility that he might lose, he didn't think it mattered. Then when he didn't win, the notion that something might happen to the *Mermaid Queen* would also never have occurred to him.

As upsetting as all of these things were, she couldn't deny that they were consistent with what she knew to be true about her papa. However, it was the story about her cousin Katherine that made her angry. This one was a little harder for her to accept. While Vida was certain if something served his purposes he'd try to see it done, she would have never believed him capable of something so underhanded. But even that seemed to have turned out well for everyone involved. What angered her was that he had never told her about Katherine. He had hidden the fact that she ever existed by refusing to allow her to be mentioned.

If what she was feeling in this moment was anything akin to what her father felt when he lost his temper, she could understand why he lashed out. She wanted to scream at him and tell him that if the mess they were in right now didn't prove how dangerous it was to hide the truth, he deserved every bit of it.

But she wasn't her papa. She would maintain her self-control. Besides, for the first time in her life, she had to keep a secret from him at least for a little while. The fact was, his decision to ask Tomas to marry her and lead Clan Ruthven was perhaps one of the best he'd ever made. She loved Tomas and he loved her but more importantly, there was no single person who could do a better job leading the clan than the two of them together. Tomas respected her and would allow her to continue doing what she did best, managing the clan business. And he would continue to build their men into a formidable force and provide for the protection and safety of their people. Then, too, there was the fact that he already felt a devotion to the clan, something that someone who married her for the title he'd inherit might never have.

Somehow in the midst of what might have been a disaster, by the grace of God, her father had managed to stumble on the perfect solution to ensure the clan's wellbeing for years to come. She wouldn't allow his short-sightedness to ruin that.

So, when her father asked her to join him in his solar, she listened to everything he had to say, reacting appropriately with shock and horror when it was required. When she cried, an easy enough thing to do considering all that had happened, he begged her forgiveness. When she moaned, "What are we going to do? What's to become of me?" he offered his solution.

"You'll marry Sir Tomas MacHenry, on the Feast of Saint John the Evangelist. He's already an excellent leader of our men and he'll be a good husband for you. We'll post the first banns on the twelfth of December."

"And that will solve the problem?"

"Aye, if you're already married by Hogmanay, there's nothing Lindsay can do but negotiate with me for the final amount I owe."

He didn't mention the fact that Lindsay could possibly move to stop that wedding and force full payment of the debt. He also didn't mention that if the marriage went ahead as planned and he couldn't pay all he owed, Lindsay could conceivably lay siege. It disappointed her that he was not being fully honest, even now. But as a result, she didn't feel guilty for not telling him she knew these things could happen as well as the fact that she and Tomas had discussed it and had made plans accordingly.

"Vida, my love, you will agree to marry him, won't you?"

She nodded. "Aye, Papa, I will." He looked so distraught it tore at her heart. She knew he'd brought it all on himself, but he was her papa and loved him. "Papa, don't look so sad. This might be the best thing that could ever have happened. You're right about Tomas's abilities and the truth is, I quite like him." She smiled. "And I'm rather certain he likes me too. It will be a good marriage."

Her father heaved a sigh, looking relieved. Perhaps more relieved than he should. "Excellent. We'll announce it at the evening meal."

Her eyes narrowed and she canted her head. "I'm not certain that's the best idea."

He frowned. "Why not?"

"Well, it just seems to me that we don't want to risk Lindsay hearing news of the wedding."

"Who would tell him?"

"I don't know, Papa. I just don't think we should take the risk."

"The banns have to be posted anyway."

"I know, but you plan to post them on the twelfth. After that there are only fifteen days for news to reach his ears. If we announce it today, there are twenty-six days."

Her father shrugged. "I don't think we need to worry, but if you want to wait until the twelfth we'll wait."

"Thank you, I think it is safest."

"It won't leave us much time to plan a great wedding feast."

"Papa, you owe a huge debt that you can't pay. I don't think now is the time to make extravagant expenditures."

"But the ship from Venice…"

"Will arrive when and if it does. If ye wish to have a celebration then, we can. But it's irresponsible to spend money we don't have." She looked pointedly at him and could not hold back the next comment. "We wouldn't be in this mess if you'd remembered that in August."

He hung his head. "I'm sorry, Vida."

She smiled and ducked her head down, so she could meet his eyes. "Just don't do it again…ever."

Her father remained subdued for the rest of the day. He was surprised to learn that Tomas had sent Ethan and Drew home.

"They'll come back as soon as they can." Then Tomas added in a low voice so as not to be overheard, "I really should have sought my laird's permission to marry before I agreed to it. I have to at least tell him before the wedding occurs."

~ * ~

Keeping the secret for eleven days had been harder than Vida imagined. Once she knew she'd be marrying the man she adored, she wanted to tell everyone. She wanted to be able to hold Tomas's hand in public or to not worry about someone discovering them in the midst of a stolen kiss. So, it was a huge relief when on Sunday the twelfth, her father announced the betrothal during morning Mass.

She had argued with him all week about how much to tell the clan. Vida wanted him to tell them about the debt, their current financial distress, and why the sudden marriage was necessary.

He insisted that they didn't need to know all the details. It would only worry them.

On Saturday evening, she had wielded her final weapon. "Papa, by not telling them you are tying my hands. It leaves me unable to ask what I need to of them in order to make what funds we have last. They must know. They must understand why economies are necessary."

"They're necessary because I say they are," he roared.

She stood her ground. "You will *not* take that tone with me. I have never been one to lay blame. It usually serves no purpose. Problems are often caused by a combination of things and creating a scapegoat doesn't solve anything. But in this case, there is one source and one source only for where we find ourselves and that is *you*, Papa. You did this. The clan will pull together and help us save funds if they know why we must."

"Maybe it won't be necessary, the *Merry Mistress* might—"

She slammed her fist on the arm of her chair, cutting him off. "Nay! You made a foolish wager with money you didn't have. You didn't ensure that a betrothal to me was absolutely not an option. You didn't tell me about the risk until it was too late for me to make certain we had adequate funds. No one else is to blame."

"Vida, pet, I know it's my fault, but why do we have to tell the clan."

"Because they deserve to know. They have a price to pay, just like I do."

"I thought you wanted to marry Tomas."

"That's not the point. Papa, it will be much better for our people to hear this from you and to hear your remorse. But I swear to you, if you do not tell them why all of this is happening, *I will*."

His posture stiffened. "I forbid you."

"Forbid me, will you? Then I'll tell you the consequence you haven't even given a thought to. What is the reason for most hurriedly arranged weddings?"

His mouth was set in a stubborn line and he didn't answer.

"The answer is pregnancy. And when a nobleman marries his daughter suddenly to one of his guardsman, everyone will assume it's because I'm not a pure bride. They'll think I'm already carrying a child. And I mean *everyone*. All of our people, all of your peers, even the king."

"But you're not expecting. Everyone will know that soon enough."

"Are you honestly that blind? Of course, I'm not with child now, but I could become so on our wedding night. Then tongues will be wagging and people will be counting on their fingers. Are you willing to put me through that? Do you care for me so little?"

"Nay, Vida, my precious lass, you are everything to me."

"Then don't make me bear the brunt of ridicule for your mistakes."

And that was the weapon that felled him.

He gave a long, defeated sigh. "Fine. I will make it all public."

So, when he stood before the people during Mass, he confessed everything that happened, he asked for the clan's help over the next few weeks and months, he thanked Tomas for his assistance, and to her utter amazement, he asked for forgiveness. But having faced his transgressions so publicly, he didn't wish to speak to anyone after Mass. When Father Michael gave the final blessing, her papa practically ran from the chapel and sequestered himself in his solar for the rest of the day.

She guessed she couldn't blame him. That he had admitted everything was enough for now. In his absence, she and Tomas greeted people after Mass and accepted their congratulations and their pledges to do what they could to help.

After the last person left, Vida turned to read the banns posted on the door. She could scarcely believe it was really happening and it gave her a thrill to see it in writing. She scanned the document until she reached their names, and then laughed.

"What is it?" asked Tomas, who had been reading over her shoulder but evidently hadn't gotten that far yet.

"The names. Look closely at your name."

He leaned in and examined the parchment carefully.

Then he started laughing too. "I wondered how he was going to do that."

Father Michael had written their names in such fancy script that they were barely legible. He'd even added some extra swirls after Tomas's surname to make it appear longer, but Lady Davida Ruthven would be marrying Sir Tomas *MacIan* not Tomas MacHenry.

It wasn't obvious unless one looked closely, but clearly the priest didn't expect anyone to do that. Now that she thought about it, Vida realized when he'd read the banns aloud, before posting them, he had simply said Lady Davida and Sir Tomas.

When they returned to the keep to break their fast, a loud cheer went up from everyone in the great hall. She had been a little worried that the people who knew Tomas's real identity would disapprove. Yet many of them were in present and appeared as happy as everyone else. Still, none of them knew that *she* knew who Tomas really was.

For the rest of the week, she floated on the wave of collective joy. Everywhere she turned, everyone she spoke to was nothing short of thrilled over the news and that fed Vida's own giddiness. Of course, the fact that Tomas could touch her, hold her hand, and even steal a kiss in public—all of which he did as often as possible—might have contributed to her giddiness as well.

Then on Monday after the banns were read the second time, her world came crashing in. A messenger arrived mid-morning. Just as they had feared, word of the pending wedding reached Naughton Lindsay. She wasn't sure how. She hoped there wasn't a spy in their midst. The fact was, her wedding was the talk of the village. The story might simply have been spread by a passing tinker or merchant who had over-heard a bit of juicy gossip.

Vida's father took the message to his solar alone, but within a quarter of an hour, he'd sent a servant to find her, Manus, Gregor, and Tomas.

She and Manus were the first to arrive. He bade them sit then said no more, staring morosely into the fire in the hearth. When Gregor and Tomas arrived, clearly fresh from the training field, Ambrose turned to address them.

He waved the paper in his hand. "I have just received a missive from the Lord Sheriff in Perth. I have been summoned to appear before him tomorrow, to answer charges filed by Laird Lindsay on behalf of his brother Naughton." He looked down at the paper. "Naughton believes that we entered into a verbal agreement promising Vida's hand to him should I be unable to pay the debt I owe him by the end of December. He has reason to believe that I cannot pay said debt, and yet I have announced my daughter's pending nuptials to someone else. He is demanding that I repay the loan immediately or that the sheriff uphold the previously agreed betrothal."

The room was silent. Vida stood and wrapped her arms around her father.

He returned her embrace, trembling. "I'm sorry, Vida. I'm so sorry."

"Everything will be all right, Papa."

"I don't see how. The only way for you to avoid marriage to Naughton Lindsay is to enter a convent."

She wished she could tell him that he would be able to pay the debt. But she wasn't absolutely certain of that now. The MacIans hadn't arrived yet. Tomas believed they would, but Vida certainly understood why they might not.

"Laird, I will gather everything of value we have and bring it to Perth on your command. We almost have enough," said Manus. "Perhaps if you're only short a small amount, he'll give you a bit more time to pay the rest."

Her father shook his head, a tear slipping down his cheek. "I didn't realize it at first, but this has never been about the money. He wants to marry Vida and become the laird eventually. If I am short a farthing, he'll force the betrothal."

141

Vida made eye contact with Tomas. She couldn't stand to see her father defeated.

Tomas clearly understood her plea and stepped in. "Laird, all is not lost yet. When Ethan and Drew returned to the Highlands, I asked them to ask my family if they might be able to loan ye the shortfall. Clearly, no one has arrived yet with any coin, but they may still. Keep hope and I'll do what I can."

"Tomas, you have been my savior, Vida's savior, over and over. Fate seems to have turned against me, so I will not rest all my faith in a loan from your family, but I will cling to that hope. That said, Tomas, I'm putting you in charge here with the authority to act in my stead. Gregor, I'd like you to accompany me with a contingent of men. I will send messages to keep you informed. If things look like they will not go my way, Tomas, take Vida to the Highlands. I don't care where you go. Don't even tell me. I don't want Lindsay ever to find out."

"Papa, I will not desert you and my clan."

Her father gripped her by the shoulders, becoming sterner than she had ever seen him. "You will do as you are told. I will not allow you to marry Lindsay under any circumstances. If it becomes necessary, you will either go to the Highlands with Tomas or if you truly don't wish to do that, enter a convent. Those are your choices. Do you understand me?"

"Aye, Papa."

~ * ~

Within the hour, Tomas stood beside Vida with his arm around her as Ambrose Ruthven rode out of Cotharach accompanied by eight men. The irony of the situation was not lost on Tomas. He should have been savoring the sweet twist of fate that had forced Ambrose into a trap so like the one of his own making nineteen years earlier. But there was nothing sweet about this. The woman he loved was hurting and he would do whatever it took to fix this.

A tear slipped down her cheek. "I know he brought this on himself. I should be furious, but he's my papa."

Tomas kissed her head. "I know he is, sweetling. Hopefully, my family will arrive soon and we'll sort it out."

She turned toward him, wrapped both arms around him burying her face in his chest, and burst into sobs.

"Wheesht, my sweet lass. Wheesht now. Don't cry. I'll take care of things, I swear it to ye."

CHAPTER 15

Tomas had never made a promise that he wasn't certain he could keep, but as he'd lain in bed the previous night, he worried. What if, what if, what if. It made his head spin.

He believed his father would come. But what if something happened to them on the way? What if they were robbed and their coin was stolen? What if they didn't get there in time?

What if, with Laird Ruthven gone, someone seized the opportunity to attack?

What if the sheriff acted quickly and Laird Lindsay rode on Cotharach tomorrow, with a writ demanding Vida be turned over to him.

The last "what if" had been the one that filled his heart with dread. It was a distinct possibility that Tomas couldn't ignore. The only way to truly protect her from that horrible eventuality was to see her to an abbey first thing in the morning. She wouldn't have to stay long. As soon as his parents arrived and the debt could be paid, Tomas could bring her home.

And if the worst happened, if the sheriff acknowledged the betrothal, as soon as he could Tomas would steal her away from the abbey and take her somewhere safe. Aye, Saint Oda's was the best place for her. He'd see it done in the morning.

Unfortunately, that turned out to be much harder than he'd imagined. He had raised the subject while breaking their fast together and she flatly refused.

"Vida, my love, surely ye can see how dangerous it is for ye to just wait here?"

"If someone lays siege to my home, I will be here to defend it," she declared.

"Does Cotharach have a bolt hole or some other secret way out that I don't know about?"

"No."

"Sweetling, I will protect ye with my life, but that's what it might come to. Our men are much more prepared than they were two months ago, but I still can't be certain that Cotharach wouldn't fall."

Her face softened and she caressed his cheek with her hand. "I can't leave my people. Please don't ask me to."

"But if ye just go to the abbey for a few days, just until we know more about what's happening with yer da…"

"Tomas, I have spent most of my life doing whatever I had to do to keep papa on an even keel. And perhaps because of that I have always done exactly what he asked of me and what other people expected of me. Including throwing chess games to avoid injuring men's pride. But then you arrived and you wouldn't let me do that. You tell me I'm smart and that you respect me. My darling, I know you want me to go to the abbey and I understand why. But please, let this be my decision. I will go if it becomes necessary, but it isn't necessary today."

He sighed, gathered her in his arms and kissed the top of her head. "I will allow it to be your decision today. I reserve the right to change my mind if danger is imminent and you are stubborn."

She hugged him back. "I'll take that answer for today."

Well, if she wouldn't go to the abbey ahead of trouble, he would have to make certain they had plenty of warning if trouble approached. December days were short and today was the shortest of them all. The sun would set in the middle of the afternoon, less than an hour after none. So, they wouldn't be able to see anyone approaching the castle until it was too late to get Vida safely away. He wanted sentries posted far enough from the castle to ensure adequate time to prepare.

At this moment he missed Duncurra more than he ever had. Built on a crag that jutted into a loch, the castle was easy to defend and its elevation made it easier to see danger approaching.

His heart nearly stopped when one of the sentries he sent to the northwest was spotted riding back at full speed.

When the sentry arrived, he announced, "Sir Tomas, a hoard of Highlanders—at least thirty heavily armed men and maybe more—are approaching from the north."

Tomas heaved a sigh of relief. "Well, thank God."

The messenger and the other men nearby stared at him in horror. Tomas could only laugh. For the first time since the summons had arrived from Perth, the sentry bore good news…even if none of the Ruthven men knew it yet. "That *hoard of Highlanders* is my family, who I expect have the means to get us out of this mess."

Soon enough, the riders could be seen emerging from the forest.

"Sir, I think you've made a mistake. Laird Carr isn't among them," said one of the guardsmen.

"Aye, well that would be because Sir Tomas isn't a Carr," said one of the older guardsmen.

Tomas arched a brow at him. "Ye know who I am."

"Aye, sir. You're the image of your father and I considered him a friend."

"You don't know any Highlanders, Archie," said another man.

The man chuckled. "Tomas wasn't born a Highlander. He was born a Ruthven. Ye played with him when ye were a lad."

The other men's shocked expressions amused Tomas, but they were wasting time. "To make a long story short, I left Cotharach with Lady Katherine when Ambrose married her to Laird MacIan. If ye don't know that story, ask someone who's been around a while. Laird and Lady MacIan adopted me and they are almost to the village. Archie, please go tell Manus and Moyna. They'll pass the word. I'm going to find my betrothed so I can introduce her to my parents.

~ * ~

Katherine had been excited about seeing Cotharach again. Ethan had told her as much as he could about it and Clan Ruthven. Still, there was nothing like seeing it with her own eyes. The sun had set as they emerged from the forest, but it was still twilight and torches lit the top of the palisade. When she slowed her horse, Niall motioned for the company stop.

"Is something wrong, my love?"

"Nay, I just want to look for a minute." It had been nineteen years since she'd seen Cotharach and then her life had been exceedingly difficult. But seeing it now brought to mind a better time, a happier time, when her parents were both living. Cotharach had been her home and Clan Ruthven her people. Looking down at the castle and village now, she let those memories wash over her.

"I know this must be hard for you."

She smiled up at him. "Surprisingly, it isn't. I thought it might be too, but most of my life at Cotharach was wonderful. It was only the last few years, after my father died, that things got really bad. And those memories have faded, in no small part thanks to ye." She looked over at her husband, reached a hand out to him and he took it in his, squeezing lightly. "I'm ready now."

"Good. Because just before we crossed onto Ruthven land, we saw signs suggesting men are encamped in the woods. I'm anxious to reach Cothararach." Niall signaled for the MacIans to begin moving again.

"You believe men are encamped at the border and you didn't check it out?" she asked, appalled.

"You clearly haven't been married to me long enough if you think I would risk the safety of my family to approach an unknown group of men in the forest."

She smiled. "I've been married to you long enough to know a handful of MacIan warriors is all it would take to rout an army."

"I appreciate your faith, my darling, but sometimes caution has more value than bravery. But I did send two men to scout the area to see what we might be dealing with."

It wasn't long before the entire party reached the edge of the village. Very little had changed and seeing it awakened even more wonderful memories.

Forty people on horseback don't go anywhere quietly, so as they rode into the village, clansmen and women came to their doors and opened windows to see who was riding toward the castle. Katherine's heart nearly burst as recognition dawned on many of their faces.

"Lady Katherine, look its Lady Katherine."

"Lady Katherine, child, we never thought to see you again."

Katherine's heart was filled with warmth and affection. She reached out to them, spoke, and called them by name. They were the people of her childhood and she still loved them dearly.

"What brings you back, child?" asked an elderly woman named Ana.

"Ana, how wonderful to see ye." Frankly, Katherine hadn't expected her to still be alive. She must be close to ninety years old now. "I've come at Sir Tomas's request," was all she could say. The truth of the full story would come out soon enough.

When the MacIans reached the gates, they were already opening. She rode into the courtyard and standing there on the steps of her old home, waiting for her, was her beloved son, Tomas. She could hardly dismount fast enough.

"Mam, welcome back to Cotharach." He opened his arms for his mother and folded her in his embrace.

Niall wasn't far behind her. He offered Tomas his hand, but pulled him into a hug with it. "Son, it's good to see ye."

Tomas guided forward a beautiful brown-haired lass who had been standing slightly to one side. "Vida, these are my parents, Niall and Katherine MacIan. As ye're already aware, Katherine is yer cousin."

Vida seemed shy and nervous. "Welcome to Cotharach, Laird MacIan," she bobbed a curtsy. "Lady MacIan."

"I'm not Lady MacIan. I'm yer cousin Katherine and I want a hug." Katherine opened her arms to the lass.

Vida stepped into her embrace. "I'm so very sorry for everything that happened. My papa never told me about you."

"Vida, there's no need for apologies. None of this is your fault. I'm just glad we're finally able to meet."

Behind Vida and Tomas waited old friends. Manus had been the steward for as long as Katherine could remember and Moyna, the woman who ran the kitchens, had aged, but looked well and hearty. Emma, who had been Katherine's maid, was there as well with tears in her eyes. When Katherine had left Cotharach, Emma had been barely fourteen and she had cried that day too. Katherine greeted them all with hugs and tears.

"My lady, I can scarcely believe it. I thought I'd never see you again," said Emma, tears still streaming.

Katherine laughed. "If I recall correctly, you were certain the Highlanders would kill me."

Emma chuckled. "Well, clearly I was wrong. You look wonderful. Happy."

"I am happy. As much as it pains me to admit this, Uncle Ambrose, having arranged my marriage to Laird MacIan, was the single greatest blessing of my life."

"Mam," whispered Beitris who had dismounted and stood beside her.

"Oh, good heavens, forgive my manners." Caught up in greeting her old friends, Katherine had failed to introduce her children. "Lady Vida, everyone, these our other children. Beitris, James, and Alex."

Tomas ruffled James's hair. "I'm surprised to see you here."

"Laird MacLennan sent word to Laird Matheson as soon as he heard what was happening here. Laird Matheson intended for me to go home for the Christmas season, but knowing Mam and Da would be coming here, he sent me home a little early."

Tomas glanced beyond them. "It looks like Drew and Ethan are helping sort things out with the men," he motioned toward the doors, "so there's no reason to take a chill standing on the steps, please come into the hall."

Stepping into Cotharach's great hall was like stepping into her childhood. The last few years she'd lived here, Uncle Ambrose had been miserly and refused to spend money on any comforts. But now the hall was once again well-appointed and brightly lit, just as she remembered it from when she was little. It warmed her heart.

"Mam, Da, please join us at the table. Supper is nearly ready to be served."

Niall put his hand in the small of Katherine's back, and guided her toward the laird's table. He leaned down to her ear and whispered, "This is an entirely different reception than I received last time."

She arched a brow at him. "That's because last time ye were a huge stranger with a scowl that appeared permanently etched on his face and I was weak in the knees with fear."

He chuckled. "And now?"

She grinned. "Now, you're my huge husband who only has an occasional scowl etched on his face and who makes me weak in the knees for much more wonderful reasons."

"Cheeky lass."

She laughed.

When they were all seated at the table and before the servants started serving the meal, Tomas stood to address the clan. "I realize many of ye don't understand exactly what's happening, so if you will indulge me for a moment, I'll tell ye. My name is not Tomas MacHenry. I am Tomas MacIan. I am the adopted son of Laird and Lady MacIan. Some of you may recognize Lady MacIan as Laird Ainslie Ruthven's daughter, Katherine."

A buzz of murmurs filled the great hall as those gathered for the meal processed what Tomas had just said.

"Furthermore, knowing that, some of ye may realize I was once a stable boy here until I left with Lady Katherine."

The murmurs and exclamations of surprise grew louder.

"Have you come to take back what is yours, Lady Katherine?" the question was not asked with malice, rather the old man seemed excited by the prospect.

Katherine laughed. "Nay, Hamish, Cotharach it is not mine and I am very happy at my new home. I understand my Uncle Ambrose is currently in the midst of some financial distress and we may be able to help him."

A huge cheer went up in the hall.

When it had quieted some, Katherine added, "And we've come to see our son, Tomas, married."

Another huge cheer erupted.

Katherine looked with fondness at her son where he sat smiling, holding Vida's hand.

"They look as if they'll be very happy," said Katherine.

The response to that statement was deafening. Vida dropped her head slightly, blushing, but looked exceedingly happy and that gave Katherine great joy.

During the meal, the men who Niall had sent to scout the forest arrived and were shown into the hall. They wore grim expressions and spoke quietly to Niall.

Niall, in turn, shared what he'd learned. "Tomas, son, we discovered something as we rode onto Ruthven land this evening that I must discuss with you."

Katherine was pleased to see that Vida scowled at that and even more pleased with Tomas's response.

"Da, Vida is Lady Ruthven and if something threatens her clan, she has the right to hear about it."

Niall cast Katherine a sidelong glance. "Aye, well it's rather clear then that she's related to your mother. But, as ye've surmised we discovered something that concerns me. We saw signs of men encamped in the forest at the northern border of Ruthven land."

"That would be Stewart territory," said Vida.

"Aye. But I sent a couple of men to learn what they could. They tell me there were at least fifteen men and a Lindsay banner was spotted."

Vida nodded. "Stewarts and Lindsays are allies."

Tomas frowned. "It's as I feared then. Lindsay is moving his men into place to either lay siege to Cotharach or make certain Vida doesn't leave."

"I suspect so," agreed his father.

"I'll send twice as many patrols out tonight. Better to know where they are, should we need to defend against them."

CHAPTER 16

Perth, December 22, 1378

Ambrose Ruthven paced his small bedchamber furiously. The only accommodations that he'd been able to arrange were in a somewhat seedy tavern that had seen better days. He accepted them at the time assuming he would only be in Perth for a night or maybe two before the issue was resolved. After all, the sheriff had summoned him to appear *immediately*. But he had spent two nights there already and he still didn't know when the sheriff would hear the case. Maybe today, maybe tomorrow. Ambrose had washed, dressed, and eaten something to break his fast. Now all he could do was wait.

As patience had never been one of his strengths, waiting was not something Ambrose did well.

Finally, by midmorning, word came that the sheriff was ready to hear the case. Ambrose's temper by this time was foul. Gregor rode beside him and as they neared the court, he said, "Laird, I know this has been stressful for you. I know you are angry at having to wait so long. I don't wish to make you angrier, but I feel I must say something."

"Then say it," growled Ambrose.

"You are going before the sheriff. I'm certain Laird Lindsay will come prepared with witnesses to your conversation. I fear you're only going to have reason to grow angrier."

Ambrose glanced sideways at him. "I'm not sure where you're going with this, but *you* are making me angrier."

"I'm sorry, Laird, I'm only trying to point out that if you go into court this upset and you lose your temper to an even greater degree, you will also lose any chance you have of the sheriff showing you the slightest bit of compassion. Please, Laird, for your sake, Lady Vida's sake, and for the sake of the entire clan, you must try to calm down."

Ambrose clenched his jaw and looked away. He knew Gregor was right. "I don't know how," he ground out.

"I think you need to imagine Vida is standing behind you."

Ambrose sat there for a moment, shaking his head. "Aye, you're right. If Vida were here, this would be easier. I'm probably too old to play pretend, but I'll try."

It still took ages before the sheriff was ready to hear the case. As they waited, some part of Ambrose clung to the hope that Lindsay really just wanted his money back and it hadn't been about a betrothal to Vida. Then he saw the men who stood with Lindsay. Of course, his brother, the Laird, was there. Additionally, Laird Ogilvie, several of his sons, and Laird Rattray were with him. To his surprise so was Laird MacNab. Ambrose smiled when he realized Laird Gow wasn't there. The reason was probably because Tomas had showed some leniency to Gow's men after the raid. But Lindsey had enough other witnesses that it didn't really matter.

The Lord Sheriff called the assembly to order. "Gentleman, we are here today to discuss a case of indebtedness. Laird Ruthven, a complaint has been filed against you by Laird Lindsay on behalf of his brother, Naughton. He alleges last August during a game of chance you borrowed a considerable amount of gold from Naughton."

"Aye, that is correct," agreed Ambrose.

"He further alleges that you guaranteed said loan on a shipment of goods expected from Genoa."

"Aye, that is also correct."

"Has this shipment of goods arrived?"

"No, it has not. But the loan in question doesn't come due until the last date of December."

The sheriff addressed Laird Lindsay. "Is this true?"

"I will allow my brother Naughton to address this question."

"Sir Naughton, is this true?"

"Aye, it is true, however, I have reason to believe Laird Ruthven's shipment from Genoa will not arrive. Other ships bound for Genoa, that left port well after Laird Ruthven's ship did, have long since returned. And the captains of those vessels report that Ruthven's vessel, the *Mermaid Queen*, never arrived in Genoa."

"But Laird Ruthven may be able to make good on the debt without the income from that vessel. If you agreed to allow him until Hogmanay to pay the debt, he has not yet defaulted."

"That is true," agreed Naughton. "However, Laird Ruthven and I had a verbal agreement, witnessed by all of these men who were present that night," he motioned to Lairds Ogilvie, Rattray, and MacNab, "that should he not be able to pay his debt, he would give me his daughter's hand in marriage."

"I did not agree to that. My Lord Sheriff, Naughton made a jest about my daughter's hand, but I did not agree to it."

"Were these other men present as Sir Naughton says they were?"

"Yes, but I thought it a jest. I would never have wagered my daughter's hand."

The sheriff frowned. "Gentleman, you were all present the night in question?"

All of the other men confirmed this.

"And do you believe, as Sir Naughton does, that Davida Ruthven's hand was part of the bargain or was it a jest?"

Ambrose was not surprised that they all agreed with Lindsay.

The sheriff nodded. "In the absence of a written agreement, I can only make a determination based on witness testimony. Laird Ruthven, while you may have interpreted Sir Naughton's comment as a jest, I find in his favor that should you be unable to pay your debt, a betrothal to your daughter will be given in lieu of payment. But in so doing, all parties have already agreed the loan has not come due yet."

Naughton gave a slight bow of his head. "That is true, my lord sheriff, but I have recently learned banns have been posted announcing Davida's pending marriage to someone else. I suspect Laird Ruthven is unable to pay what he owes and he is trying to circumvent our agreement by this hastily arranged wedding."

Ambrose couldn't hold his tongue. "There is nothing hasty about it. After all, everything is being done in the open. As you said, the banns were posted."

The sheriff shook his head slowly. "Perhaps, but the timing is suspicious. To whom is she betrothed and for how long?"

"She is betrothed to the commander of my men, Sir Tomas MacHenry. They have known each other for a while now and are very much in love."

Laird Lindsay barked a laugh. "Are you trying to tell us you are marrying your daughter to one of your men? And this isn't a convenient way to avoid making good on your debt?"

Ambrose shook his head in angry frustration. "As it happens, the young man is one of the finest warriors I have ever encountered. He is a natural-born leader and a better man to one day hold the title of Laird of Clan Ruthven than any I've ever known." He took some satisfaction in Naughton's affront. "Furthermore, anyone who knows me knows how precious Vida is to me. If I can make her happy and secure skilled leadership for my clan, I will do that."

"But you can't do that. She is betrothed to me until you pay the debt," roared Naughton.

The sheriff arched an eyebrow. "Hold your tongue, Sir Naughton. This is my court."

The fact that the sheriff wasn't immediately falling to the whim of the Lindsays encouraged Ambrose a little.

The sheriff addressed him. "Laird Ruthven, I accept that your motives for the wedding seem reasonable. However, the timing still remains suspicious. But this can all be solved rather simply. Do you, or do you not, have the funds required to pay off the loan?"

Ambrose waffled. "I still have over a week to pay my debt."

"That is not what I asked. Do you have the funds, at this time, to pay off the loan?"

"My lord sheriff, even if I do not have the golds at present, that doesn't mean I won't have it in a week's time."

"Laird Ruthven, my patience is wearing thin, you will answer the question I asked."

Ambrose heaved a sigh. "I have nearly all the gold necessary to make good on this loan."

A triumphant smile spread across Naughtons face. "*Nearly* isn't *all*."

"Sir Naughton, I will not warn you again," said the sheriff. Then he addressed Ambrose. "Are you expecting funds from some source before the end of next week?"

Ambrose shook his head. He didn't want to give too much away. He certainly didn't want the Lindsays to be watching the northern road for Highlanders bearing gifts. "There is a chance my other ship might arrive…or something else might happen."

"How much are you lacking?"

"I have enough to pay eighty to ninety percent of what I owe. And should I not have the money by the end of December, I would happily renegotiate the remaining amount and pay additional interest if Laird Lindsay is willing."

The sheriff turned towards Laird Lindsay. "Are you willing to renegotiate? After all, it is a significantly smaller amount."

Laird Lindsay puffed out his chest. "No, I certainly am not. I am owed what I am owed. Laird Ruthven has had more than enough time to ensure he could pay off his debt. I am under no obligation to extend him further credit. He will pay what he owes, or he will agree to a betrothal between his daughter and my brother."

The sheriff sat quietly for a few moments clearly deliberating on what he had heard. He gazed around the room as if taking the measure of every man present. "Gentlemen, there's a great deal at stake here. I would be remiss if I made a judgment too hastily. I would like to take some time to think on this further, so we will to reconvene tomorrow and I will render my decision at that time. Until then, Laird Ruthven, I find that your daughter is not free to marry. And, in the intervening hours, I strongly urge you to find someone willing to loan you the shortfall."

"Yes, my Lord Sheriff." But if Ambrose were honest with himself, he believed there was very little hope of that. Regardless of what Tomas believed, there was absolutely no reason why his parents would loan money to a man they didn't know. He had only one option now. He would send a messenger back to Cotharach and instruct Tomas that if his parents hadn't arrived, he should escape with Vida to the Highlands.

CHAPTER 17

Cotharach, December 22, 1378

It had been two days since Vida's father had left for Perth. In the surprise and bustle of the MacIans' arrival yesterday, she had been busy and hadn't stopped to worry about what might be happening with him. Meeting her cousin Katherine had been wonderful. Learning from their patrols that Lindsay men were encamped on Rattray land to the southeast and MacNab land to the west had her nearly sick with worry. But foremost in her thoughts today was her father. When he left on Monday, she figured there might be a chance he'd return yesterday but barring that, she expected him today at the very latest. When one of his men-at-arms arrived alone in the afternoon, her heart fell. The man had requested to speak to Tomas privately.

Tomas had taken her hand and said, "This concerns Vida more than anyone. She'll hear this message with me."

"But, Sir Tomas, the laird—"

"—left me in charge. Vida will stay to hear this."

It had actually been a relief to hear the Lord Sheriff had delayed the case, but the fact that he accepted Lindsay's claim about the betrothal was distressing. Clearly, her father didn't believe Tomas's parents would arrive to help. Thus, fearing the case wouldn't end well, he'd sent instructions for Tomas to flee with her.

"Vida, my love," said Tomas, "don't worry so. As I knew they would, my parents brought enough gold to help with the debt. This will all be resolved tomorrow."

Even now, Tomas, a number of Ruthven men, and the even more MacIan men were preparing to leave at first light. They would be transporting the full amount of gold needed to pay the debt. They couldn't risk encountering thieves by traveling after dark or with anything less than a large force of skilled warriors.

"But, Tomas, you'll have to pass through Rattray land where the Lindsays are encamped in order to reach Perth."

Tomas assured her all would be well. "We'll be traveling with a large force of well-trained men."

Still, Vida couldn't help but worry and she said as much to Katherine at the evening meal.

Katherine smiled warmly. "I know ye're worried. Ye can't help but be. Still, I can assure ye, the MacIan men are among the best warriors in the Highlands. They will be able to handle anything that arises."

"That's good to hear. And if Tomas, Ethan, and Drew are any indication, I have to believe you."

Katherine patted her hand. "But believing me and letting it ease yer mind are two different things."

Vida nodded. "I'm also worried about Cotharach's protection. Our men at arms have vastly improved since Tomas arrived, but I'm concerned."

"What worries ye?" asked Laird MacIan.

She frowned. "Well…I guess…I like playing chess. And sometimes, one must draw one's opponent's attention away from one's own plans. It has become clear that Naughton has his eye on gaining Cotharach and Clan Ruthven for his own. But he can't be assured that Papa won't be able to pay the debt or that someone won't come through with another loan, just as ye have. So, if he really wanted Cotharach, drawing Papa away and then attacking from three sides would be one way of catching us off-guard."

Both Tomas and Laird MacIan gave her admiring looks. Laird MacIan said, "Very well-spotted, Vida. You must be an excellent chess player."

"Ruthless," said Tomas with a laugh. "And ye're right, Vida, it is a possibility."

This didn't exactly calm her fears.

"But, my love," continued Tomas, "Da and I have discussed this. If ye approve, I'll leave him in charge of the men here while I go to Perth. He is an experienced warrior and leader—no match for the handful of Lindsays encamped around us. Cotharach will be in good hands."

She nodded. "That makes me feel a bit better."

Just then, one of the guardsmen who had been on duty at the gate entered the hall with a Trinitarian priest and a young boy of about twelve. He escorted them to the head table. "My lady, Sir Tomas, this Red Friar and the lad with him have a tale you must hear immediately."

Vida nodded. "Certainly. Father, I'm Lady Vida Ruthven. This is my betrothed, Sir Tomas MacIan, and his parents Laird and Lady MacIan."

"I'm very pleased to meet you all. I am Father Owen and this lad is Will."

The boy was slender, had tanned skin, white-blonde hair, and deep blue eyes. He bowed and greeted them, "Pleased to meet you my ladies, Laird, Sir Tomas."

Vida smiled. "Join us at the table and have some supper as you tell your story, Father."

"Thank you, my lady. However, I can only tell a small piece of it. Most of it is Will's to tell." They were seated and the priest continued. "As you can see by my scapular," he pointed to the red and blue cross on the outer garment of his habit, "I am a priest in the Order of the Most Holy Trinity. Our charism centers on redemption and mercy. From the very earliest day of our order, we have been devoted to the mystery of the Holy Trinity and the ransom of captives held by nonbelievers. Although rooted in the Crusades, most of our work now involves gaining freedom for the victims of piracy who have been sold into slavery."

A chill passed through Vida. "*Piracy?*"

"Aye, my lady. And the story we bring you, concerns your father's ship, the *Mermaid Queen*."

"It was pirated?"

"Aye, my lady."

Horrified, Vida's hand flew to her mouth. "Oh, dear God." She glanced around. Lady Katherine seemed equally upset. Tomas and his father wore grim expressions.

"But God is good. I and some of my brothers were in Tangier, working to gain the release of other captives, when we learned of a Scottish ship that had been sailed into port, and sold along with all of the crew members."

"You were able to save them?" asked Tomas.

The priest shook his head. "Not immediately. We did not have enough funds to secure everyone's release but we brokered an arrangement with the slave trader who bought them. My brothers paid the man a sufficient amount for the sustenance of the crew for sixty days, during which time the order would acquire the funds needed to purchase the crew's freedom outright. We had some remaining funds, approximately enough to purchase three men. However, the captain insisted that the coin be used to secure the release of young Will here, the ship's cabin boy. You see, men who are sold into slavery are used for forced labor. The fate of women and children who are forced to be slaves is usually far worse. And the prices they bring are often significantly higher. Captain Lowther feared that if a buyer offered enough coin, the slave trader would sell Will in spite of the agreement with us. Because I am a Scotsman, I agreed to accompany the lad back home."

"When did this happen?" asked Tomas.

"In August. It has taken us a while to get here. First it was necessary to travel to Spain so that the brothers there could begin gathering the funds to ransom the remaining crewmen. Then we had to wait until we could book passage to England or Scotland. We finally arrived in Edinburgh three days ago. We went first to the Red Friar's Abbey in Scotlandwell, then came here. But I'll let the lad tell the rest of the story. I assure you, they were not set upon by typical pirates."

The boy had been eating hungrily while the priest talked. Vida couldn't suppress a smile when Will swallowed what was in his mouth, took a drink from his goblet, then wiped his face with his sleeve before launching into his tale.

"The *Mermaid Queen* left port at the end of June and the first leg of the journey went well. We arrived at the port in Cadiz, Spain, at the beginning of August. The captain took on fresh provisions and water there. We were only in port a few days before setting out again. To Captain Lowther's surprise, there was another ship from Dundee, the *Salty Swan,* already in port when we arrived."

Vida frowned. "The *Salty Swan*? That's one of Naughton Lindsay's ships and it left Dundee after the *Mermaid*."

"Aye, my lady, it did. Our captain knew that too. He even talked with the *Swan's* captain who said he'd left port on the next tide but managed to make better time."

Vida shook her head. "But that's not true. It left days later."

"Aye, my lady, after all that happened, that doesn't surprise me. She was riding high in the water when we were in port as if she were nearly empty. Captain Lowther thought her contents must have been sold in Cadiz and that the *Swan* would be taking on goods there. We left Cadiz as planned. We were only hours out of port when sails were spotted behind us. We assumed it to be another merchant vessel, but it was too far away to identify her. By evening, as we set a course towards the Strait of Gibraltar, the ship began to gain on us. The lookout and first mate said she was a Portuguese merchant ship. I didn't think so. She was fast, and high in the water, like an empty ship. I found the captain in his cabin and told him what I'd seen. He ordered me stay in his cabin while he went on deck. Before long, from the captain's porthole, I could see the other ship coming along side. It was the *Swan*. I heard fighting on the deck but it didn't last long. It turns out six of our crewmembers, including the first mate, had been

bribed by the captain of the *Swan*. They overpowered
Captain Lowther and the Quarter Master, drugged some of
the seaman and assisted the captain of the *Swan* in taking the
ship."

"You were pirated by Lindsay's ship?"

"Aye, Sir Tomas. Our crew was shackled and locked
in the *Mermaid*'s hold. I heard some of the *Swan*'s men
arguing with their captain over this. Apparently, he was
supposed to murder the entire crew to ensure no one would
ever learn what had happened. But he said if he sold us into
slavery, we'd never see Scotland again anyway and it was
foolish not to take the money we'd bring. So, men from the
Swan piloted the *Mermaid*, and both ships made port in
Tangier the next day. Then, the *Mermaid*'s cargo was
transferred to the *Swan*. It had been empty from the time it
left Dundee. That's how it made such good time. The captain
of the *Swan* sold the *Mermaid* to a Moroccan merchant. Then
he sold the entire crew, including the men who betrayed us,
to a slave trader."

"And were your brothers eventually able to gain the
men's freedom, Father Owen?" asked Vida.

"Aye. The coin was taken to Tangiers before Will and
I left Spain and I received word that they'd been released."

Tomas shook his head in disbelief. "I can't believe
the *Swan*'s captain turned on the men who helped him."

His father shrugged. "He'd have to. Lindsay was
clearly behind this. He couldn't risk a single crewmember
ever returning to Scotland. Especially not men who had
already demonstrated that their loyalty could be bought. If
they'd turned on one master for a price, they'd turn on
another."

Will nodded. "Aye, that's what the *Swan*'s captain
said." He cast a sidelong glance at the priest. "I thought they
deserved what they got, but the Red Friars ransomed the
whole crew."

Father Owen chuckled and ruffled the boy's hair. "Will's learning it's sometimes hard to understand the nature of God's mercy."

Niall MacIan laughed. "The truth is, lad, by rescuing them, in spite of what they'd done, those men will always bear the guilt of their betrayal. Perhaps they'll be less tempted to ever do it again."

"Aye, that's what Captain Lowther said too. Most of the men argued with him but he stood firm, saying he didn't condone revenge. He said if the men returned to Scotland, he would seek justice for their crimes." The boy frowned. "I don't understand the difference. It seems right just to me for them to have to suffer the fate they led us to."

Lady Katherine smiled. "The difference between revenge and justice is hard to understand, Will. Let me ask ye this, if another lad yer age called ye a rude name, what would ye do?"

"I'd tell him he was an eejit and he ought to shut his fat gob."

Her eyes sparkled with amusement. "And would he? *Shut his fat gob*, that is?"

Will's brow drew together. "Probably not. He'd probably say something worse to me."

"And you'd say something worse back and so on. But how would it end?"

"I don't know. A fight I guess."

Katherine nodded approvingly. "I suspect so. I have sons and that is the usual progression of silly arguments. But ye see, it's a constant spiral down. One person hurts another. Then the other person wants to hurt the first one a little bit more. And it just keeps on going like that. But justice is different. It's fair, rational, and brings closure. Letting an impartial judge decide the punishment for their crimes helps ensure that it will be fair."

"Doing to them what they were planning to do to us seems pretty fair to me."

Katherine laughed. "Still, ye aren't really impartial now are ye?"

"Nay, I guess not. But what if they don't come home?"

"If they don't come home, it will be because they fear the crown's justice, not the captain's vengeance, therefore, they have essentially condemned themselves to exile. You see it wouldn't be Captain Lowther, any of his men, or the Red Friars who are forcing them to stay away. It'd be their own guilt."

"I suppose I understand that."

Tomas had been watching his mother with something akin to awe on his face. "Mam, the way you do that has always amazed me."

"Do what?"

"Explain things that aren't always easy for little ears to understand."

"Oh, that. I learned it from yer father."

Niall shook his head. "Ye didn't learn it from me. I'm not very good at it."

Katherine laughed again and flashed Niall a cheeky grin. "No, I don't suppose ye are, but 'twas from helping ye see my point of view that I learned it."

Niall chuckled, "Aye, well, that's entirely possible."

Katherine smiled at Vida. "And men aren't all that different from wee lads sometimes. Vida, I expect ye've learned the same thing over the years from Uncle Ambrose."

"Be that as it may," said Niall with mock sternness, "We have a problem to address."

Tomas nodded. "Aye, we do. It appears that Lindsay has been working for some time to lay this trap. If he sent his ship on the heels of the *Mermaid Queen* in June, that was weeks before Ruthven incurred the debt."

All of the implications of that began swirling in Vida's brain. "So, Naughton entered into a game of chance with Papa, and when Papa was losing, allowed him to secure a debt with goods from a ship that would never reach its destination."

Tomas shook his head. "I doubt there was ever any 'chance' involved in that game. There is no way of proving it, of course, but it's likely that Lindsay cheated to ensure yer father incurred a significant debt."

"Yer probably right," said his father. "What's more, if he has put so many components in place to secure this victory, the chances that he has nothing else up his sleeve are slim. This makes Vida's earlier concerns additionally worrisome. He might have more men on the road between here and Perth than we know, waiting to ambush Ruthven men who might be transporting a large amount of gold. Ye can be certain he won't leave this to chance, so it's likely to be a sizable force. He may even have more of his troops waiting in places we've yet to discover, prepared to attack Cotharach."

Tomas nodded. "I suspect ye're right, Da. In Laird Ruthven's message to me, he wanted me to flee with Vida. Clearly if I had done that, I'd also have met Lindsay men on the north road."

"So, what are we going to do?" asked Vida.

A broad grin spread across Tomas's face. "We'll give them no cause for alarm. We no longer need to transport the funds to Perth. If Father Owen and Will present what they know to the sheriff, Lindsay will be the one facing justice. And any men he might have lying in wait along the route won't give a second look to a farmer, a priest, and a young lad traveling to Perth."

Vida frowned. "Are ye sure that's safe? Why not just travel with a sizable contingent of men anyway?"

"Because warriors will most definitely draw their attention, which would likely end in a battle," answered Laird MacIan. "And that would put Father Owen and Will at risk. Tomas is right, they'll pay no attention to a priest, and two peasants. And that will leave a much stronger force here to guard Cotharach."

Tomas addressed the priest. "Father Owen, will ye and Will accompany me to Perth?"

"Aye, of course," said the priest.

"Then we'll go by wagon at dawn."

Vida laid her hand on top of Tomas's hand where it rested on the table and gave a squeeze. "Thank you, Tomas, for everything you've done for us. Katherine and Niall, I can't thank you enough either. After learning some of the ugly truths about my father, I would have understood if you'd turned your back on us."

Tomas pulled her hand to his lips and kissed it. "This is about much more than your father. I could never let ye or this clan pay the price for his wrongdoing."

"None of us could," added Katherine.

Having the support of Tomas and his parents touched her beyond words. Naughton Lindsay had made a series of calculated maneuvers that would have ruined Clan Ruthven and left her in his control. And to make things worse, her father had been far too easily manipulated along the way. That frightened her more than anything else.

When she retired to her chamber that night, she couldn't free her mind of the fear gripping her. Even though all of their problems seemed to be resolving, they had skirted so close to disaster, it chilled her to her core.

Something had to be done to ensure nothing like this could ever happen again and it couldn't wait until Tomas returned with her father from Perth. In fact, that might be too late. It needed to be addressed right now.

She rose from her bed, put on a dressing gown, and, taking a candle, slipped out of her chamber into the dark, quiet corridor. She walked resolutely to Tomas's room and tapped lightly on his door.

Tomas opened moments later, wearing only a tunic, but a sword in his hand. "Is something wrong? What's happened?"

"Nothing has happened. Nothing new anyway. But I need to talk to you."

"Vida, this isn't exactly proper," he said, even as he opened the door wide to let her in.

She stepped into the room. "I know it isn't. What I'm about to ask you probably isn't either, but it won't stop me."

His eyebrows shot up and a slow smile spread across his face. "Well, make yerself comfortable. Can I pour ye a goblet of wine?"

A goblet of wine. That was exactly what she needed. "Yes, thank you."

He poured two goblets of wine from the ewer that stood on his table and handed one to her. "Will ye sit down, my love?"

"Aye, thank you." She sat in one of the chairs at the table, and fortified herself with two long swallows of wine.

He frowned, taking the seat opposite her. "Something's worrying ye."

Vida nodded. "Aye. I think we need to get married."

Tomas laughed. "My darling lass, we are getting married."

"I mean tonight."

"Ye know Father Michael will not marry us until the banns have been announced for the third time."

"I know. But we could handfast, here, right now."

"Vida, there is no longer any fear of ye being forced to marry Naughton Lindsay."

"And that is exactly my point. My father made a series of terrible decisions that landed us here. The one good decision he made was to ask you to marry me. But thanks to the greed of the *Swan*'s captain, everything has turned out in my father's favor. I fear, once he realizes he has been miraculously extricated from this mess, and he finds out who you really are, he'll change his mind about our wedding."

A pained look crossed Tomas's face. "I suppose that's his prerogative."

"But it would be the wrong thing to do. And I would live in fear of him doing something like this, only perhaps even more dangerous in the future."

"I understand, really, I do. And I want to marry ye. But ye must know, it's likely to infuriate him. Are ye prepared for that?"

"Aye. I am."

"Then there is one other thing to consider. Even if we are married, that doesn't prevent him from endangering the clan's well-being in the future."

She frowned. "I know." She leaned across the table and grasped his hand. "And while I hope, between us, we can exert a bit more control, that isn't my main reason for wanting to handfast tonight."

"Then what is yer main reason?"

She felt the color rise in her cheeks and glanced away for a moment embarrassed. But she'd gone this far, she had to finish it. She returned her gaze to his. "I love you. I love everything about you. You are a skilled warrior and a good leader. But you are also kind, compassionate, and generous. I love being with you. I can be myself without worrying that you won't approve. And what's more, I'm confident that you love me too."

The look on his face was priceless and worth every bit of the effort it took to say all of that.

"Vida, my precious lass, I do love ye, with everything in me."

She looked down, fighting tears. "But I'm so afraid Papa will ruin everything again. I can't risk losing you, Tomas. I don't think I could stand living without you."

~ * ~

Live without her? Nay, Tomas couldn't do that. "Oh, sweetling." In one swift move, he pulled her off her chair and into his lap. "Although I'd thought about the possibility, I didn't think your da would do that. Your happiness seems to be very important to him. But ye're right, he doesn't always make sound decisions and ye know him better than anyone. I won't risk losing ye either. Of course, I'll handfast with ye."

He felt her relax in his arms and she nestled against him. She had truly been terrified.

"Do we need a witness?" she asked.

He chuckled. "I'm not sure. I've never handfasted with anyone before."

She smiled up at him. "I haven't either. But if we are doing this to ensure Papa doesn't stop the wedding, I figure we should have someone who can serve as our witness."

Tomas nodded. "I could ask Drew or Ethan, but I figure if we choose a friend of mine yer father might not believe they tell the truth. We should choose someone who yer father respects."

"Aye, ye're right. We should ask Manus. Papa respects him and Manus respects you. If it never needs to be revealed, he will keep our secret, but he will stand by us."

"Then Manus it is. I'll go fetch him."

She shook her head. "Nay, let me go. He will want to ask questions of me to make sure you aren't exerting some sort of pressure. I will be better able to convince him if we are alone."

"I'd rather go with ye, but if ye think it's best I'll wait here." He helped her off his lap and walked with her to the door.

"It won't take long, I'll be back in a few minutes."

His chamber was dark and chilly, the fire having been banked for the night. It lent a clandestine atmosphere to the whole thing that Tomas didn't like. So, he lit several candles and stoked the fire to warm the room. He also wrapped himself in a plaid. He wouldn't marry her half-dressed.

Then he waited.

And waited.

He guessed it hadn't been all that long, but it felt like eons. He had time to think about what they were doing, but he didn't change his mind. Vida had been right on all counts. He had feared as much, but hadn't allowed himself to think of the possibility of not taking her as a wife.

So, by the time Vida returned with Manus, Tomas's resolve had only been strengthened.

Vida's face was alight with a smile. "Manus has agreed to be our witness."

Tomas took her hand, kissing the back of it. "Excellent." To the small, sleep tousled man in her wake, he said. "Thank ye, Manus."

"'Tis an honor, Tomas. And make no mistake, I love Vida as a daughter. I want to see her happy and I know she will be if she is married to you. Even so, I would not normally go behind my laird's back to see it done. However, I firmly believe Vida is right about her father and the risk he poses to the clan. You are, without a doubt, the best man to lead us. Therefore, as it is in the clan's best interests, I will witness this. I hope the wedding will take place in a few days and no one ever needs to know. But if something goes awry, we'll do what we must."

Tomas nodded. "I appreciate yer confidence, Manus, and I swear I will do what I must to see Clan Ruthven remains safe and prosperous."

"I know you will. Now, I would like to get back to bed, so let's get this done. Ye need only state your intention to take each other as husband and wife."

Tomas turned to face Vida, taking both of her hands in his. "I, Tomas MacIan, take ye, Davida Ruthven, to be my wife until we are parted by death and I promise ye I will be true."

Vida's smile was like a beacon of light, making the candles he had lit pitifully unnecessary. "I, Davida Ruthven, take you, Tomas MacIan, to be my husband until we are parted by death and I promise you I will be true."

Tomas leaned in and kissed her softly on the lips. "I love ye, Vida MacIan."

A blush suffused her face. "I love you too, Tomas MacIan."

Manus cleared his throat. "Well, now that's taken care of, I'll return to my chamber." He glanced towards Tomas's bed. "And...uh...one last thing. Normally a handfasting should not be...uh...consummated until it has been blessed by the church. That said, an unconsummated handfasting can be set aside, but once consummated it cannot." He smiled, inclined his head in a slight bow and left.

As the door closed behind Manus, Tomas grinned. "I think we've just been instructed to have our wedding night a bit early.

She giggled. "Aye, it would seem so."

He pulled her into his arms and gave her another kiss. She melted against him, wrapping her arms around his neck. Her warm response pleased him. "Is that what ye wish to do? I mean, I don't want to push ye, if ye aren't ready."

She answered him by pulling him down into another kiss.

"Ye're so beautiful," he said as he ran his hands softly over her back and down her sides, ending the journey by cupping her breasts in his hands. "And ye taste so sweet." He continued the gentle assault on her mouth, sliding his tongue over hers then lightly sucking on her lower lip. He opened her dressing gown. She wore only a silk shift. He gently rubbed his thumbs over her nipples, feeling them pebble beneath the soft fabric. She gave a low moan, leaning into his touch.

He slid the dressing gown over her shoulders, allowing it to puddle on the floor. Then he kissed her again as he untied the ribbons of her shift, pushing it over her shoulders and off. Stepping back, he gazed at her for a moment. "So beautiful," he repeated.

She flushed under his gaze, but made no move to cover herself. Instead, she unbound her hair from its braid before stepping back towards him. "Ye have me at a bit of a disadvantage." She removed the plaid he had donned so hastily, dropping it on the pile of her clothes.

Her small hands roamed over his chest and shoulders; the feather-light touch inflamed him even through the fabric of his *léine*.

He too explored her body with his hands, scarcely able to believe she was his.

She gave a little shiver.

"Ye're cold."

"Nay, I just like the way that feels."

He lifted her into his arms anyway and carried her to the bed, laying her gently on it. "Still, ye'll be warmer here." But he couldn't help taking a step back to simply gaze on her again. She was a vision. Her hair a silk cushion under her delicate, lushly-curved body. He drank in the exquisite sight and, although her blush deepened, she didn't look away from him. "My lovely bride, ye please me so." She smiled and her green eyes sparkled.

He pulled off his *léine,* smiling when he heard her soft intake of breath. Climbing into bed beside her, he pulled the covers up over them both and gently stroked the length of her body, planting soft kisses on her face. As she relaxed into his touch, his lips moved to her neck, making her purr with pleasure. Then he continued his journey to her silky shoulder, before finally capturing a nipple lightly with his mouth and suckling gently.

As he continued to gently lave her pert nipple, she murmured, "Mmmm, I like that."

"I thought ye might." His hand trailed down her stomach until he reached the nest of curls hiding her womanhood. "Ye might like this too." His fingers stroked her softly, and he smiled at the slightly surprised look on her face.

Within moments, she closed her eyes and writhed against him as he massaged the sensitive spot between her legs. Her breath came in short gasps. He could feel the tension building in her, so he stopped.

Her eyes flew open. "Why did you stop?"

"Because, my beautiful bride, anticipation makes everything better." He kissed her and began caressing her again. He set a pace that had her arching towards him, wanting more, but not quite enough to allow her to find release. She looked as if were lost in some other world. It was the most erotically beautiful sight he'd ever seen.

Finally, when she had hovered on the edge so long he knew the slightest change in touch would send her over, he knelt between her legs and entered her. Her eyes flew open, but if she felt any discomfort, it didn't show. She rose to meet him.

"Oh, Tomas…"

Her frenzied movements drove him to increase his pace.

"Let it go, Vida," he whispered and she shattered in his arms, crying out his name again. As the waves of her climax shuddered through her body, Tomas too found his relief, filling her with his seed. Panting, he rested his forehead on hers and whispered, "*Vida.*" It was almost a supplication.

He shifted his weight to the side and held her to him, still joined.

She ran her hands lightly down his arms and across his chest. He captured one of her hands in his and kissed her fingertips. "Are ye all right?"

"Oh, aye. More than all right." Her voice sounded breathless.

"I didn't hurt ye overmuch?"

175

She looked confused. "Hurt me? Nay." She frowned. "But it's supposed to hurt a lass, isn't it?"

Pleased, he chuckled. "Not if ye do it right."

She gave him a wicked grin. "Well, I won't ask where ye learned, but clearly ye do it right."

He pulled out of her gently and she turned on her side, snuggling against him, her head resting on his shoulder. He buried his face in her hair, inhaling deeply. "I love the feel of ye in my arms."

"I love being in yer arms. I hate to leave."

He kissed the top of her head. "Why would ye leave?"

She sighed. "Because if I wait until morning, I'm likely to run into someone. We're keeping this a secret for a few days, remember?"

He groaned. "Oh, Vida, I'm sorry. I don't like the idea of ye sneaking back to yer chamber, as if we've done something wrong. But I wouldn't see ye shamed for anything."

"It will only be a few days and I'll sleep in your arms every night for the rest of our lives."

"Aye, my love. For the rest of our lives."

CHAPTER 18

Perth, December 23, 1378

That morning Ambrose Ruthven had received word that the sheriff would reconvene court an hour before sext. Now, just as they had yesterday, he and Gregor waited for the sheriff to call them in. Ambrose hadn't slept at all the previous night. He was tired and his heart ached. He had likely lost his precious daughter. She was probably well on her way to the Highlands by now. He might never see her again and he hadn't even been able to say goodbye.

When the sheriff finally assembled all parties, he asked, "Laird Ruthven, I must ask again, were you able to secure the remaining funds needed to pay your debt to Laird Lindsay?"

Ambrose shook his head. "Nay, I was not. Not as yet."

The sheriff nodded. "Well then, Laird Ruthven, given that you do not have sufficient funds to pay your debt and you are not expecting additional funds to arrive before the debt is due, I can only agree with Laird Lindsay. The wedding of your daughter before a debt on which you are very likely to default is due is an attempt to circumvent the verbal agreement."

"But, my Lord Sheriff—"

"Do not interrupt me. Therefore, I am forced to rule that a betrothal exists between your daughter and Naughton Lindsay and she is not free to wed anyone else."

The look of glee on Naughton's face sickened Ambrose.

"But, Sir Naughton," qualified the sheriff, "you may not act on that betrothal until after the first day of January and if, by some miracle, Laird Ruthven is able to pay you the full amount he owes before the last day of December, a betrothal will no longer be valid."

Laird Lindsay blustered, "The man has already admitted he cannot pay the debt, my brother should be allowed to take his bride immediately."

The sheriff's eyes narrowed in anger. "Laird Lindsay, make no mistake, I understand perfectly what happened here. Marriage to Davida Ruthven brings with it a title and lands any man would covet. I do believe Laird Ruthven thought your brother's comment was a jest and perhaps if the men present as witnesses that night had not all been your close allies, they might agree with me. Therefore, I am taking the remainder of the agreement at face value too. The debt has not yet come due and until it does or it has been paid off, Lady Davida Ruthven will marry no one. However," he turned his attention back to Ambrose, "If you are unable to pay your debt and you do something to prevent the wedding, you will go to debtors' prison. And I will petition the king to grant your lands and title to Naughton Lindsay."

The Lindsays were jubilant.

Ambrose was stunned. He had just lost everything. As soon as he received word that Davida had indeed fled to the Highlands with Tomas, he would board one of his ships and flee Scotland.

Then a voice sounded from behind him. "Excuse me, my Lord Sheriff. I have some information that you will want to hear."

Ambrose turned around to see Tomas had entered the hall, accompanied by a priest and a young boy. His heart fell. If Tomas was here, he hadn't taken Vida to safety. "What are you doing here?" he demanded. "You had orders."

"Aye, sir, but this will change everything."

The same called for order. "Who are you and what is this new information? Has the missing ship arrived?"

"My lord, I am Sir Tomas MacHenry, the commander of Laird Ruthven's guard and nay, the *Mermaid Queen* will never return."

"You are the man to whom Laird Ruthven intended to marry his daughter?"

"Aye, my lord."

"And how do you know what happened to the *Mermaid Queen*?"

"I was placed in charge of Cotharach when Laird Ruthven was called to appear here. Yesterday, this Trinitarian priest, Father Owen, and this young lad, Will, arrived at Cotharach with tale of such treachery it boggles the mind. Ye see, sir, Will was the cabin boy on board the *Mermaid Queen*. According to him, the ship was pirated by none other than the captain of the *Salty Swan*, one of Naughton Lindsay's ships."

Everyone in the room began talking and shouting. The sheriff's voice carried over all the others calling for order.

Ambrose was dumbstruck. Tomas had saved him once again.

When the sheriff was finally able to bring the proceedings to order, he listened to the story Will and Father Owen told. He asked questions and shouted down the Lindsays several times. In the end, he sat speechless, seemingly stunned by the story.

Finally, he addressed Naughton Lindsay. "Do you have anything to say in your defense?"

"It's all lies. I had nothing to do with any of this."

"Are you suggesting, based only on your assertion, that I should believe a holy priest fabricated this story and is lying to me? Don't dig a deeper hole by perjuring yourself. The lad was on the ship, and Father Owen witnessed the sale of the rest of the crew to a slave trader. He also spoke to Captain Lowther, who tells the same story as the lad." He turned to Laird Lindsay. "Were you aware of your brother's perfidy?"

"Nay, my lord, I was not."

"Well then, regarding Laird Ambrose Ruthven's debt, while I suspect that your brother may have cheated to arrange the whole gambling loss, I have no proof of that, so the debt stands. But I am ordering it be deducted from the total value of the goods pirated and the lost ship. The remaining funds will be returned to Laird Ruthven. Any perceived betrothal between Naughton Lindsay and Davida Ruthven is now void. Additionally, I am ordering you, Laird Lindsay, to supply the Trinitarian's with every farthing that was required to free the *Mermaid Queen*'s crew and return them home to Scotland. Furthermore, I am declaring the captain and crew of the *Salty Swan* guilty of piracy and ordering their arrest should they ever be found on Scottish soil. Finally, Naughton Lindsay, I find you guilty of conspiring with pirates. Piracy itself is punishable by death, but the decision as to what becomes of you belongs to the crown. I am ordering that you be detained in the king's prison until such time as the king can hear the particulars of this case."

And with that it was over.

Ambrose could scarcely believe it. The debt had been eliminated, there was no longer any threat to Vida, and he would even be reimbursed for the loss of his ship. He embraced his young commander. "Tomas, how can I ever thank you? You are my savior, the best thing that ever happened to Clan Ruthven. Come let's get out of here." Ambrose turned and walked towards the door.

~ * ~

Tomas followed Laird Ambrose until they were outside, surprised to hear Ambrose start to blather on about the money he'd lost. "Now, if you could just figure out how to get that gambling debt back from Lindsay...I shouldn't have had to pay that cur anything. I'm certain he cheated. He doesn't deserve a single farthing of it. We'll put our heads together and maybe we can figure out a way to get that gold back."

Tomas listened to Laird Ruthven with incredulity. The man's greed knew no bounds. Now was the time. He had to step in for Vida and the good of the clan.

"Laird Ruthven, by the grace of God, ye will neither be destitute nor will yer daughter have to marry a man as reprehensible as Naughton Lindsay. But it has taken ye mere minutes to begin scheming a way around the Lord Sheriff's judgement. Ye've already forgotten how very close to disaster ye brought the clan, not to mention the callous disregard ye showed Vida."

"Disregard? I didn't...I never."

"Stop. Ye did and ye know ye did. This didn't happen by accident. Ye were greedy. Pure and simple. Ye thought ye had the chance to win a huge bet and that was the only thing guiding yer actions that night. Ye were so certain of winning, ye wanted that loan at all costs. Look into yer conscience, man. Ye can't tell me ye believed Lindsay would have given ye the loan if ye'd pushed back about the betrothal."

"I...I..."

"Ye know I'm right."

"But everything worked out."

"That doesn't excuse what ye did," roared Tomas.

"Nay, but..."

"There are no 'buts.' Ye have not been a good leader for Clan Ruthven. Ye've left it to others to manage. First yer wife, then yer steward and yer daughter. Had ye never sought that loan, ye'd still be in dire straits at this moment because ye didn't see to the training of yer men. In fact, I suspect if Lindsay hadn't been able to trick ye into a betrothal with the loan, he would have laid siege by now. Cotharach and yer title were always his goal. If he'd done that, ye and many of yer people would be dead and yer daughter would be in that bastard's hands."

Ambrose paled. "I thought…that is…I gave it my best effort."

"But ye didn't. Ye said as much to me. Ye said ye weren't trained to lead the clan, Ainsley was. Ye built a successful business and continued to put yer focus there even after ye had wrested the title of laird for yerself."

"How do ye know—"

"I just do."

"Fine, but why are ye berating me? You don't need to worry about it anymore. We don't have to rush this wedding. You don't even have to marry her. In fact, it might be better if I sought a betrothal with a nobleman."

Tomas simply stared. Vida had seen this coming. It was no wonder the lass couldn't be bested at chess. She read men's moves.

"Aye, a nobleman would be a good choice," continued Ambrose.

"So, what you told the clan about me being the best man to become laird wasn't true."

"Well, it was true at the time. But I should consider other options now."

"You should consider the son of a nobleman?"

"Aye, exactly. I know you're fond of her and she's fond of you, but politics are politics." The expression on Ambrose's face suggested he was pleased Tomas saw the wisdom of that.

Tomas chuckled. "Well, laird, I have a bit of a surprise for ye then."

Ambrose smiled. "Another surprise? I can't wait to hear."

"Really? That's good to know. I won't make ye wait then. I am not Sir Tomas MacHenry, one of Laird Carr's guardsmen."

"What? You lied to me? You are not a knight?"

"I am most assuredly a knight, and I was born Tomas, son of Henry, but I was adopted at the age of seven."

"Ah, well, that really doesn't make a difference then, my boy. Whoever adopted you must have seen what a fine man you'd become."

Tomas couldn't suppress a smile. It was probably wicked, but he was enjoying this. "I'm glad you think so."

"But why did you hide this from me."

"Because ye know my parents. Ye know my mother very well. And I thought if I told ye who she was, it might change yer mind about me."

A look of shocked realization crossed his face. "You aren't…you couldn't be, could you? Are you Moibeal's son by Raghnall Napier? The one who supposedly died as a child?"

Tomas shook his head. "Nay, Laird. I'm not Moibeal's son, back from the dead. That would make Vida my half-sister and I never would have agreed to marry her. Besides, I've already told ye, my father's name was Henry. Nay, I am the son of a stable hand, but I was adopted by Laird and Lady *MacIan*. My mother was born *Katherine Ruthven*."

The range of emotions that played across Ruthven's face was almost amusing. "*MacIan?*"

"Aye, Tomas MacIan."

Shocked, Ambrose Ruthven sputtered, seemingly unable to form words.

The wickedness in Tomas simply couldn't resist toying with the man. "Surely ye remember my parents. After all, my mother is yer niece. As a matter of fact, many years ago I was yer *stable boy*."

Ruthven continued to bluster. "Of course, I know who Katherine is. Is this her idea of revenge? All this time, you've just been seeking vengeance?"

Tomas shook his head. "Absolutely not. If I had wanted vengeance, if I had wanted to see ye ruined, I wouldn't have lifted a finger to help ye. I would have gone back to the Highlands with Laird Carr and left ye in the mess ye'd created for yerself. On the contrary, the reason I stayed is because I love my mother and she loves this clan. She would not have wanted me to abandon ye, even to yer own stupidity."

Ruthven's anger was rising. "You tricked me. You tricked me into giving you Vida's hand."

"I have done no such thing. As I said, I never would have stayed in the first place had it not been for my connection to the clan and Lady Katherine's love for them. And 'twas ye, yerself, that begged me to stay and be yer commander...and then to marry yer daughter. I can walk away now if ye wish."

Tomas knew his words hit the mark. Ruthven was still angry, but he was weighing the cost of acting rashly. "Laird Ruthven, you wanted me to marry Vida when you thought I wasn't a nobleman, but not only am I nobleman, I have ties with numerous strong Highland clans. I love yer daughter and she loves me. And then there's the fact that I have an affection for your clan that no other man you choose for Vida will ever have. But make no mistake, I will not stand by as yer commander and watch ye marry her to someone else."

"You're a MacIan," he growled.

"Aye, I am. And if ye're honest with yerself, ye must admit the only reason ye're angry now is because yer pride has taken a serious blow. But even though ye mistreated Lady Katherine and bought her inheritance, no one argues that everything worked out for the best. She and Da are very happy, I've had a wonderful life, ye were able to marry the woman ye loved, and ye have a daughter whom ye adore."

It was as if that knocked the wind out of Ambrose. He looked chastened, diminished somehow.

Tomas simply stared at him, finally saying, "Whatever ye decide to do from here on is up to ye."

"Of course, it's up to me. I am Laird Ruthven and ye'd do well to remember that." Then, almost petulantly he added, "What would you have done if Father Owen hadn't arrived with Will? Would ye have done as I asked and fled to the Highlands with her?"

Tomas smiled, ready to deliver the final blow. "That was never necessary. Until Father Owen arrived, we were planning to bring the funds ye owed Lindsay to Perth today."

"But there wasn't enough."

"It's true ye didn't have enough on yer own, but before ye left I told ye I had sent word to my parents. They arrived the day before yesterday with enough gold to cover the shortfall."

Ambrose looked stunned. "Katherine is at Cotharach? Vida knows about her?"

Tomas nodded. "Aye."

"And she'd have done that for me? She'd have finished paying the debt?"

Ambrose was pitiable really. He had no sense of honor and loyalty, qualities the MacIans had in abundance. "Aye, Laird. She'd have done that for her family and clan." Tomas turned and walked away.

"Where are ye going?"

"I have an errand to run before we leave Perth. Be ready to go in half an hour."

CHAPTER 19

Vida had been on edge all day. It had started the
moment she left the warmth of Tomas's arms to return to her
own chamber. Not that she had a single regret about
handfasting with him. She was certain she'd made the right
choice. Still, sneaking around in the dark of night didn't sit
well. It left her feeling worried and tense. Then, too, she
didn't want to be right about her beloved father. Sadly, when
he returned from Perth that evening, she knew she had been.

The news was good, his men-at-arms were jubilant,
but her father was morose and Tomas didn't appear overly
pleased either.

Vida adopted a joyous demeanor, hoping it would
lighten her father's bad mood. "Papa, I'm so glad you're
home. I trust after Tomas arrived with Will and Father Owen
everything was resolved?"

"Aye," he practically grunted.

Then she noticed that Will was climbing down off the
wagon that Tomas had driven, but Father Owen didn't seem
to be with them. "Where is Father Owen?"

By this time Tomas had reached her side. He gave her
a kiss on the cheek before answering. "The sheriff ruled that
Lindsay had to pay the Red Friars the full amount required to
ransom the crew of the *Mermaid* and return them home. He
stayed in Perth to see to those arrangements. Then he'll
return to the abbey in Scotlandwell."

Vida smiled at Will, who stood slightly behind
Tomas.

As if reading the unasked question, Tomas said, "Will
is an orphan. Father Owen was going to take the lad back to
the abbey until the friars could find a home for him, but
given what Clan Ruthven owes him, I said we'd take
responsibility for him."

Just as Tomas had read her expression, Vida knew exactly what he was suggesting. After all, his life had changed forever when the MacIans adopted him. "Of course, we will." She opened her arms to the boy. "Welcome home, Will."

The worry which had been written on the lad's face transformed to shocked surprise. Then, with a shy smile, he stepped into her arms and she hugged him.

Her father scowled but said nothing.

She gave him the smile that nearly always melted his bad temper. His frown softened, but she hadn't completely calmed his mood. Unfortunately, she suspected her next announcement wouldn't help things either. "Papa, did Tomas tell you his parents have arrived from the Highlands?"

Again, a disgruntled, "Aye," was his only response.

She cast a questioning look at Tomas.

He nodded. "I told him who they were and that they'd brought enough gold to help cover his debt. Although I'm sure we're all thankful that wasn't necessary."

Ambrose snorted and strode past her into the keep.

She turned and hurried to follow in his wake. Tomas and Will following after her.

She caught up to her father and slipped her arm through his elbow, feeling some of the tension leave him at her touch.

He patted her hand absently.

Niall and Katherine sat near the hearth with their children and Vida walked towards them. A slight hesitation in her father's step told her that wasn't precisely where he had planned to go, but he let her lead him.

Niall stood as they approached. His sons followed suit.

Vida smiled broadly at them. "Papa, I suspect you remember Laird Niall MacIan."

"Aye, of course I do." His tone was gruff, but he extended a hand to Niall. "You're looking well. Thank you for coming."

Niall took his hand but there was very little warmth in his tone when he said, "Certainly, Laird Ruthven. I'm glad everything has worked out."

Katherine stood and opened her arms, stepping towards her uncle. "Uncle Ambrose, it's good to see ye."

He allowed the embrace, patting Katherine's back a bit awkwardly.

"Clearly, ye've met Tomas. These are our other children, Beitris, James, and Alex. My dears, this is yer Uncle Ambrose."

Beitris curtsied and both boys gave a small bow.

Her father seemed momentarily confused. "You have sons."

Katherine smiled. "Yes, Uncle, I do."

He frowned. "I don't have sons. That makes your sons my heirs."

She shook her head. "Nay, Uncle, it doesn't. Vida is yer heir. Niall relinquished my claims to Clan Ruthven when we married."

"He relinquished *your* claim, but if I have no heirs they are still my nephews."

Katherine's voice grew a bit stern. "You do have an heir, Uncle Ambrose. I am not here to claim an inheritance that isn't mine. Vida is yer heir and I will never contest that."

He looked confused again. "Then why did you come back?"

"Because my son, Tomas, said ye needed our help."

"Why would you want to help me if not to take back your inheritance?"

Vida was shocked. "Papa! Stop this."

Both Tomas and Laird MacIan looked ready to do battle.

Katherine put up a hand. "Uncle Ambrose, whether ye believe it or not, I care about this clan. I care about my cousin. And I care about ye. I don't need anything from ye and I don't want anything from ye."

Her father stared at Katherine, for a moment then seemed to relax a little. "I'm sorry. Thank you for coming. You'll excuse me now, it's been a long day." He pulled away from Vida and strode towards the exit to the stairs.

"But, Papa, supper is ready to be served." Vida called after him.

"Send a tray up."

Vida turned back to her guests. "I'm so very sorry. I've never seen him behave like this."

Katherine patted her arm. "Don't let it upset ye. I'm sure the last few days have been exceedingly stressful and finding me here when he returned didn't help."

Tomas scowled. "Mam, ye and Da only came to help. There was no call for what he just did."

"Tomas, he expects others to be as grasping and greedy as he is," said his father.

Upset, Vida looked away to gather her composure. Laird MacIan's words were harsh, but she couldn't deny the truth in them. "I fear, ye're right, Laird MacIan, but I expect, after he's had a chance to calm down and rest a bit, he'll realize he's made a mistake. Please, join me at the table now for supper."

During the meal, Tomas filled them all in on everything that had transpired in Perth.

After the trial, Tomas had sought out Laird Lindsay to suggest he remove his men from the Ruthven border. "The news that the Ruthven garrison had been reinforced by a *hoard of Highlanders* convinced him that any attempt to wrest Cotharach from the Ruthvens would end in crushing defeat. So that threat has been removed as well."

As it turned out, Will had paid particular attention to the court proceedings. He had noticed Lindsay's allies had physically distanced themselves from the Lindsays when the tide turned against them. "Captain Lowther always says rats leave a sinking ship. Now I understand what he meant."

Will had also apparently been in awe of the fact that the sheriff held the Lindsays responsible for the funds the Trinitarians paid to gain the crew's freedom. He told them stories of the wonderful work the Red Friars did. "My lady, the thought of being sold as a slave—well, I can't tell ye how scared I was. I'm glad they'll be able to save others."

Vida decided to speak to her father about making a substantial donation as well.

Later that evening after she had retired, to her absolute delight, Tomas came to her chamber. As soon as he was through the door, she flew into his arms.

He captured her lips in a hungry kiss. She gave herself over to the wonderful sensations it awoke in her and was left a little dazed when the kiss ended.

He chuckled, "I'm glad to see ye missed me."

She felt her cheeks redden, but she grinned and said, "It seems you missed me too."

He nuzzled her neck. "Oh, I did. I missed ye dreadfully."

She giggled and reached for the belt holding on his plaid. "Then we must waste no more time."

Tomas shook his head and took hold of her hand. "Nay, lass. I fear we have things to discuss first."

She frowned. "Nay. I'm fairly certain I won't like the things ye have to tell me. I think it would be much better to enjoy ourselves a bit first. Then we can talk about serious matters."

"Ah, lass," Tomas kissed her. "How can I argue with that? Ye're a brilliant strategist."

"I'm glad you agree. Now, where was I?"

He took a step back, holding out his arms. "I believe ye were divesting me of my clothing."

She smiled broadly. "Yes, of course, how could I have forgotten?" She unbuckled his belt, removing his plaid. Then she began to unlace his tunic, planting kisses on his chest.

"Ye're torturing me lass." He scooped her, laughing, into his arms. He kicked off his shoes before laying her on the bed and taking a moment to remove the rest of his clothing.

As he undressed, she rose onto her knees and removed her dressing gown. She was left wearing nothing but her silk shift.

Tomas, in his naked glory, leaned forward, planting kisses over her face and down her neck as he pulled at her shift, tugging it up, over her hips. He stopped kissing her. "Raise yer arms for me, lass." She did and he pulled the shift up and off. He stopped and stared at her. "I have never seen anything more beautiful than ye are at this moment, Vida."

She felt a hot blush rise under his perusal, as a wave of shyness passed through her, her hands fluttered up, covering her breasts.

"Nay, my bonny lass, let me savor yer beauty for a moment." She dropped her hands to her thighs and looked into his eyes. The look of desire she saw there was indescribable. She felt adored.

Tomas climbed on the bed beside her. Capturing her lips again, he kissed her passionately. When he released her lips, she panted, breathless. He kissed her neck, then nuzzled behind her ear, causing her to giggle. He gave a low, throaty chuckle and, sliding her hair out of the way, planted kisses around to the back of her neck and then down her back. She shivered and gave a throaty moan. When he reached the base of her spine, he planted kisses around and over the curve of her hip. "Lay back, sweetling."

Vida shifted off of her knees and rested back onto the bed. He kissed his way across her belly and up to her breasts.

His hands roamed freely over her body before cupping her breasts and brushing his thumbs gently over the peaks. She too explored his body with her hands. When she trailed her hands down to his hips and over his buttocks, he groaned.

"Ah, lass, I can't bear it."

He touched her between her legs, stroking her. Just as it had the previous evening, his touch sent her to another world. She was aware of nothing around her, only the incredible sensation growing at her core. She wanted more— she needed more. She raised her hips toward him.

"Hungry, are ye?"

Unable to form words, she could only moan her response.

He teased and stroked, bringing her ever higher.

"Please…Tomas…please."

"My beautiful lass, I can deny ye nothing." She was vaguely aware that he had moved to kneel between her legs. His hands slid under her hips, lifting her. Then, he entered her with one firm stroke, and she was lost. The building heat exploded and waves of bliss washed over her as the muscles at her core contracted repeatedly around him. With a low groan, he too found his release.

Vida wasn't sure how long they laid there, but she realized it hadn't been long enough when he lifted his weight off her and moved to lay at her side. She snuggled close, not ready to be parted yet.

His hand cupped one breast and he nuzzled her ear.

"Mmm. I could stay like this forever," she crooned.

He kissed the top of her head. "Ye'll get no complaint from me."

She closed her eyes, content to doze in his arms.

He kissed her again. "My beautiful, brilliant, strategist, I fear ye may have miscalculated this."

She chuckled and twisted in his arms to face him. "Nay. I may be guilty of procrastination, but I'm still sure it will be easier to hear what ye have to tell me now."

He smiled and kissed her lips. "I don't doubt it. I'm not sure it will make it any easier for me to tell ye, but here we go. As ye thought he might, once yer da realized there was no longer an urgent need for ye to marry, he suggested that we didn't have to rush into anything."

Tomas told her everything he and her father had discussed. "In the end, he didn't say he'd call off the marriage."

She frowned. "But he didn't agree that we could still be married."

"Nay, he didn't."

Vida sighed heavily. "Then there is only one thing to do."

Tomas arched a brow at her. "Carry ye off to the Highlands with me?"

She chuckled. "Nay. But he needs to think ye would and that I'd go. Tomas, I love him, but every day I see more and more, which forces me to admit he's not a good leader. We can't risk him doing something equally as stupid in the future."

"How do ye suggest we prevent that? What do we do?"

She gave him a sad smile. "*We* don't do anything. I have to do it. He loves me. If he'll listen to anyone, it will be me."

"And if he doesn't?" Tomas's expression was guarded, worried.

She pulled him down to her lips and gave him a kiss meant to convey everything that filled her heart. "If he doesn't, I'll let ye carry me off to the Highlands. If I cannot get him to put the clan first after all of this, he never will."

CHAPTER 20

Christmas Eve dawned, cold and stormy, and for the second morning in a row, Vida awoke craving the warmth of the man she loved. He had stayed with her well into the night. At some point, they had made love again and she had fallen asleep cuddled against his chest. But later, he must have slipped away because now he was gone. Her chamber was cold. Freezing rain and ice pellets pounded the shuttered windows.

Ah well, she wasn't looking forward to the discussion she intended to have with her father and the stormy weather suited her mood. She climbed out of bed, dressed quickly, and rather than stoking the fire in her hearth, she hurried downstairs to the warmth and bustle of the hall.

It was still very early, so the last person she expected to see already up was her father. But to her surprise he sat at the table. "Good morning, Papa."

"Good morning, Vida, my darling. I was hoping to have the chance to speak with you before anyone else awakens."

This did not bode well at all. "Of course, Papa." She joined him at the table.

He had a goblet of wine in front of him, from which he took a long swallow. She waited for him to speak, knowing that pushing him wouldn't help anything.

Finally, he said, "Vida, you must realize that given all that happened in Perth yesterday, our situation has changed."

"Aye, Papa." *We no longer face a fate worse than death*, didn't seem to be the right thing to say…yet.

"Aye, well, I've decided, we needn't rush into a marriage for you. I'm calling off the wedding."

Vida sat back and stared at him. "You're doing what?"

"The wedding. I'm calling it off. The crisis has been averted. You don't need to marry Tomas anymore."

Vida stood up and walked towards the door to the entryway and the stairs.

"Where are you going?" he demanded.

"To your solar. This is not a discussion that should occur in the great hall."

"There is nothing to discuss, Vida. You will not marry Tomas MacIan."

She turned towards him, a rage unlike anything she'd ever felt burned so brightly in her she could only stare. When she finally spoke, her voice trembled with fury. "There most certainly are things to discuss. And if you hold even a modicum of love in your heart for me, you will come with me to your solar. *Now*."

Her father simply looked at her, wide eyed, his mouth gaping. If she wasn't mistaken, he was a little frightened and, by God, he should be. Without saying another word, he stood and followed her.

Good. He understands what's at stake here.

Vida's anger calmed a little as they walked in silence, but only a very little.

When they reached his solar, she lit several candles against the early morning gloom. Finally, she turned to face him.

He spoke first. "Now, Vida, my darling, you need to understand I must do as I see—"

Vida put a hand up. "Stop right there. This ceased being about *you* a long time ago."

"But Vida—"

"Nay, not another word until I've had my say. For years, I have run the business of this clan efficiently and we have been prosperous."

"No one's arguing that, but—"

"*Wheest*," she fairly shouted, glaring at him, daring him to utter another word.

He finally gave a little nod. "Fine. Continue."

"In all of these years, you haven't given a single thought as to what this clan needed. Worse, you paid no attention to the skills of your men, which has left us vulnerable. You accrued a colossal debt *at a game of chance*. You essentially threw away money that you didn't have, then, for some reason, didn't think it was important enough to tell me about it. And if all of that wasn't bad enough, you allowed Naughton Lindsay, that craven dog, to trick you into a betrothal with me. We were a breath away from disaster when Tomas MacIan, a man who has no reason on earth to want to help you…" at his affronted look she added, "don't even pretend to be the injured party here. I know what you did to him. I know what you did to Katherine. For your information, she nearly died because of the beating you gave her."

He stood, staring. Speechless.

She shook her head in disgust and paced, for a moment trying to rein in her temper. "I've never been so ashamed of you."

That arrow hit its mark. Her father looked stunned. She softened a bit. "I love you, Papa, and I believe you have changed since then. You are no longer a man who would take a whip to a lass, or a wee lad. But that you once were, scalds me. And you cannot deny that Tomas could have walked away from us without a flicker of guilt bothering his conscious. *But he didn't*. He and his men have done in a few months what you didn't do in nineteen years. Neither did he walk away when the financial mess that you created for us was finally revealed. That too would have been perfectly just. But he elected to help us. He sent word to his parents—who *also* had no reason to assist you—but they came with enough gold to save us."

She shook her head in disgust, "And then *you* insulted them by suggesting that they had only come to claim Cotharach for one of their sons. I was *mortified*."

"But Vida, this has all been resolved now. You don't have to marry anyone."

"Nay, I don't, because I'm already married. I begged Tomas to handfast with me the night before last, before he went to Perth."

"You did what?" her father roared.

"You heard me. *I begged him* to handfast with me. I knew you'd do this. I knew as soon as Tomas saved your sorry hide, you'd forget everything and look for the next pot of gold. But not this time. I love Tomas MacIan. I love him with my whole heart. I did not want to risk losing him. I need him and Clan Ruthven needs him."

Her father waved his hand as if swatting away a pest. "A handfasting can be set aside."

She glared at him. "Not if it has been consummated. And lest you feel the need to ask, it has been."

Her father began to bluster. "You had no right—"

"—I had every right. I was the one acting in this clan's best interests, not you."

Her father threw up his hands. "Fine. You've married him. You should be happy. Why are you haranguing me?"

"Because you refuse to see how close to ruin you brought us. And I've had enough."

He frowned. "What do you mean?"

"I mean, I am married to a man I love, but it would be completely foolhardy for any man to accept the responsibility of running this clan without all of the authority that goes with it. Especially in light of the tragedy that ye almost wrought simply by overconfidence, greed, and recklessness."

"Ye'd both have the authority."

"Nay, we wouldn't. Not as long as you had complete access to clan funds and the ability to override any decision we made."

"But I wouldn't do this again."

"I'm sorry, Papa, that's not good enough. You don't have a solid record of making sound decisions and I won't place my faith in what you say you will or won't do."

"What are you saying?"

"I'm saying I have married Tomas, but I will not ask him to stay here to run Clan Ruthven in your name. I'll go with him to the Highlands."

Ambrose stiffened. "You would never abandon this clan."

She cocked her head to one side and put her hands on her hips. "Nay? Are you sure about that? Your recent actions very nearly destroyed any hope I had for happiness. And to make matters worse, you didn't trust me enough to tell me as soon as you incurred the debt. All of this might have been avoided had you done that."

"All of this would have been avoided if Naughton Lindsay wasn't a craven thief."

Vida shook her head. "And right there is proof, once more, that you fail to recognize your own role in this."

"But I didn't do anything wrong. If Naughton hadn't—"

"You didn't do anything wrong? If nothing else, you gambled with a huge sum of money and *lost*. I don't think I can risk everything I hold dear on your poor judgement."

"Vida, don't leave the clan. They need you and they love you."

Vida stared at him in disbelief. "Don't dare pretend to make this about the clan. They loved and needed another Lady Ruthven once, but you managed to get rid of her to suit your own desires."

Her father looked as if she'd struck him.

"The truth is, the good of the clan has never been your first concern. Tell me, if ye'd been able to extricate yourself from this mess by taking what gold you had, boarding a ship with me and leaving Scotland forever, leaving your clan forever, would you have done it?"

Ambrose looked confused. "Well, of course."

"Oh, Papa," She pressed two fingers into the bridge of her nose. "What if Lindsay had agreed to erase your debt and set aside the betrothal in exchange for your title and lands? Would ye have consented?"

"Aye, I would have done anything to keep you out of Lindsay's hands. Besides, I still have a thriving shipping business. We would have wanted for nothing. Vida, my darling, you are the light of my life. Please don't leave me."

"You would have traded your title and lands, our clan's welfare and my legacy, to have me remain with you?"

"Aye. Anything."

"So, would ye trade it all to *secure* the clan's welfare and my legacy in order to keep me here, with ye?"

His brows drew together. "Of course."

"Then do it."

"What do you mean?"

"Give it all to Tomas and me."

"But you will have it upon my death."

"Nay, Papa, not upon your death, but upon our wedding."

He frowned. "Ye'd accept that? Ye'd stay?"

"Aye. That would give us complete authority to lead and you wouldn't have access to clan funds."

A momentary look of horror crossed his face.

She almost laughed. "Oh, Papa. That reaction just proves you're ruled by your own greed and you always will be. You just said it yourself, you have a thriving shipping business to do with as you will. Continue to put your energies there."

"And you won't leave?"

"Nay, I won't."

He huffed, but looked relieved. "Very well."

"Then we'll have Father Michael draw up the papers this morning."

He nodded. "Aye. I'll see to it."

Vida smiled at him and crossed the room to give him a hug. "Thank you, Papa. You can make the announcement to the clan before Mass tonight."

"Mass?"

She laughed. "Aye, Mass. Have you forgotten? It's Christmas Eve."

As Vida left his solar to go back downstairs, she chuckled to herself. *Checkmate.* It might have been manipulative, but it had truly been in everyone's best interests.

Tomas was at the table when she entered the great hall.

She all but skipped across the room to him, giving him a kiss on the lips to the amusement of everyone present.

He grinned. "Ye're in a good mood this morning. Sleep well?" he asked with a wink.

"Aye, but that's not why I'm in such a good mood."

"Nay? Then what has ye so full of sunshine on such a dismal day?"

"I've had a chat with my papa this morning and he's come around to my way of thinking."

"Ye're jesting."

"Nay, I'm not. As I suspected, he was planning to stop the wedding. I had to tell him it was too late for that. And we had a huge argument, but he finally gave in. He will make the announcement this evening. He intends to grant you the title of Laird of Clan Ruthven on our wedding day."

Tomas took her hand. "I'm sorry it came to this, Vida. Ye know I would have stayed with ye, no matter what."

"I know. And I really don't think I could have left the clan. But he brought us so close to ruination I had to make the threat.

CHAPTER 21

Vida woke before the sun on the Feast of St. John the Evangelist, her wedding day. Even though she had technically been married for a few days, they were finally going to be married in the eyes of the church and her family. She could barely contain her excitement. She lay in her warm bed, thinking back over the last few days.

The Christmas celebration had been one of the most joyful that Vida had ever experienced. The clan had been thrilled to have Lady Katherine and her family *home*. But they'd been equally thrilled when Laird Ruthven announced on Christmas Eve that he would be granting his title to Sir Tomas MacIan when he and Vida were married on the Feast of St. John.

To Vida's surprise, her father had been exceedingly gracious. After the Mass of the Angels at midnight, he stood before the assembly. "I have had reason the last few weeks to consider a great many things. The work of running a clan and a successful business at the same time has proven to be quite a challenge with neither endeavor getting my full attention. The time has come to make some changes to ensure our continued prosperity. God, in His goodness, saw fit to bring Sir Tomas to us. He is a fine man and a skilled warrior, who has a deep affection for this clan. And by God's grace, Tomas and Vida have grown to love each other."

He had looked into Vida's eyes, and caressed her cheek. "Vida, my darling, I adored your mama. She was my heart and my soul. I made some choices that I'm not proud of in order to have her at my side, even if only briefly. There is no greater blessing that I can ask on your behalf than for you to share your life with a man you love."

The he had turned his attention back to the gathered clansmen and women. "Vida has demonstrated her love and commitment to this clan from the time she was but a wee lassie. Between them, I believe Vida and Tomas will lead this clan with strength, wisdom, and love. Therefore, once they are married, two days hence, I will relinquish my title as Laird of Clan Ruthven to Tomas MacIan."

Vida had embraced her father with tears in her eyes. She whispered, "I love you, Papa, and I swear to you, I'll never give you cause to regret this."

He returned her embrace, then kissed her on both cheeks. "I know you won't, my precious lass. You are your mother's daughter and I am so very proud of you."

After that, nothing could have spoiled the festivities.

Then on the day after Christmas, St. Stephen's Day, the MacIans introduced Clan Ruthven to the Highland tradition of blessing the horses and livestock. Father Michael blessed baskets of hay, salt, and oats during Mass.

Beitris explained that the blessed items should be distributed to the farmers. "They can be given to sick or injured animals throughout the year."

"I've never heard of this custom," said Vida. "Why is it done on St. Stephen's Day?"

Katherine laughed. "I hadn't heard of it either until my first Christmas in the Highlands."

Tomas nodded. "I remember Da telling me a legend that St. Stephen had a horse he loved, but the horse became very ill. Christ cured St. Stephen's beloved horse and that is why Stephen's faith was so strong."

James laughed. "Aye, but Da doesn't believe that legend do ye, Da?"

Niall chuckled. "Nay, son."

"Then why do ye bless the beasts on St. Stephen's Day?" asked Vida.

"Da says," piped up Alex, "that back in the days when heathens roamed the land, horses were sacrificed at the solstice. When Christians put a stop to animal sacrifices, the horses in the Highlands, being good Christians themselves, were exceedingly grateful and thanked the first saint whose feast day fell soon after the solstice."

Tomas grinned and added, "St. Stephen would have been an ungrateful sot if he had refused to be their patron. So it was really a case of the Highland horses picking the saint as opposed to the other way 'round. At least, that's what Da says."

Vida had laughed, but she loved the beautiful tradition. "I'm sure the lowland horses will be happy enough to share the saint's devotion."

The Christmas celebration had continued that night with another feast.

But now, the day she'd looked forward to for weeks was here. As always on the Feast of St. John, Father Michael would bless kegs of wine that morning. The wine was referred to as "The Love of St. John" and would be served later at the feast. The fact that it was to be their wedding feast was a double blessing.

A knock sounded at the door, interrupting her musings.

"Come in," called Vida.

The door opened and Emma entered, with Lady Katherine, Beitris, and a stream of servants carrying a bathtub and buckets of hot water. She spent the next few hours being bathed and otherwise pampered in preparation for the wedding.

"This is a wee bit different from *your* wedding day, wouldn't you say, my lady?" said Emma to Lady Katherine.

Katherine laughed. "Just a bit. If I recall correctly, it was an unmercifully hot day. I had a quick, cold bath, and ye kept bursting into tears."

Emma laughed. "Oh, aye, you remember correctly. Now, I won't promise not to cry later, my lady. 'Twill be like watching a daughter of my own marry."

When they were finished, Vida didn't think she had ever looked more beautiful. Over layers of silk undergarments, she wore a snow-white kirtle made of the softest lamb's wool. On top of that, she wore a rich velvet surcoat of bright blue. Her hair was arranged in intricate braids and covered with a sheer silk veil, held on by a gold circlet.

"Oh, Vida, you are radiant," said Katherine, handing her a bouquet of herbs to carry.

"Thank you. Thank you for everything."

"You are very welcome. Before we go downstairs, may I have a private word with ye?"

"Aye, of course."

When everyone had left, Katherine sat on the bed and motioned for Vida to join her.

"Vida, as was mentioned earlier, in many ways my wedding couldn't have been more different than yers, and not just because of the time of year and the weather. Ye're marrying a man ye love and together, ye'll lead this clan. I was marrying a man I'd never met, I wasn't particularly happy about it, and I was being forced to leave my home and clan."

"Katherine, I'm so sorry."

Katherine smiled and took her by the hand. "It certainly was none of yer doing, and I didn't intend to upset ye. Everything ended perfectly, even if it didn't seem to start that way. But what I want to talk to ye about isn't the way in which we're different, but the things we have in common. My mother died when I was young, as did yers. I had been responsible for this clan for years as you have been. I had no idea how to be married nor anyone to help me learn."

Vida nodded and glanced down at her hands. "Aye, that has occurred to me as well."

"So, if ye don't mind, I'd like to tell ye what I will tell my own daughter on her wedding day. Choose love. Always. When things get hard—and they will at times— remember that this is a man ye love. He might infuriate ye occasionally. He might seem thicker than a stump at times.

But he loves ye too. Remember he's a human who, like us all, makes mistakes. And perhaps the worst thing is that he might make the same mistakes over and over again."

Vida laughed and Katherine gave her a *"what can you do?"* smile.

"The fact is, you'll make mistakes too. But this is key, don't let hurts fester. If something is bothering ye, talk about it. If ye realize ye've made a mistake, apologize. There is no reason for petty misunderstandings to go on for days. I'm certain ye've had to handle Uncle Ambrose with care over the years and ye've probably decided it's better to hide some things from him. But he isn't yer husband. Tomas will be. Don't hold anything back from him."

Vida canted her head. "Even if it's for his own good? To shield him from pain or heartache?"

Katherine smiled. "Tomas is the man who will share yer bed, who will know ye more intimately than anyone on earth. I swear to ye. Together, ye can handle anything better than either of ye can handle it alone."

She'd never thought of that, but when Katherine put it that way, it seemed simple. What on earth would she hide from the man who has held her as she shattered in climax? A hot blush rose in her cheeks.

Katherine chuckled. "I see ye ken what I mean."

Vida sputtered, "I…uh…we…uh…well we were worried…that is to say—"

Katherine threw her head back and laughed. "Ye made a plan to outwit Uncle Ambrose because ye're both bright and very much in love. Did ye handfast? Niall and I wondered if ye had. We'd decided it's what we would have done in yer circumstances."

Vida smiled. "Aye, we handfasted the night Father Owen and Will arrived. We worried that once Papa's problem simply disappeared, he might change his mind about allowing us to wed. And aside from loving Tomas deeply, I do truly believe he is the best possible leader for this clan."

Katherine nodded her approval. "I think that showed great wisdom. So ye understand my point. Really, at the end of the day, if ye both always remember that ye love each other, ye never intentionally set out to hurt the other person, and ye talk to each other openly, any upsets will be mild and easily weathered."

"And that's all it takes for a good marriage?"

Katherine's brows shot up. "*All it takes?* That's quite a lot. You'd be surprised how difficult it is to love a man who's being hard-headed or thoughtless." She grinned. "But do it anyway."

Vida hugged her. "I will."

"Good. Now, we have a wedding to get to."

~ * ~

Tomas had waited in the great hall with his father, brothers, Ethan, and Drew until it was time for the wedding. At one point, his father pulled him aside for a private chat.

"Son, I'm very proud of ye. I'm not certain I would have been able to step in and aid Ruthven in the first place. But you did, out of love for your mother and the clan into which you were born. You are a better man than I am in too many ways to count. So, it is probably arrogant of me to offer ye any advice, but I will. I always believed it was my responsibility to put my clan first, to consider their needs above all else."

"Aye, Da, I know ye put the clan first."

"But I don't, son. I put your mother first. In all things. Because I know what's good for her, is good for our clan. I may be the clan's strength, but your mother is its heart and soul. In a few short days, it's become clear to me that Vida, like yer mother before her, is the heart and soul of Clan Ruthven. Be their strength. Be their shield and defender. But always treat as precious what's most important to them. If ye're loyal to their lady, they will follow ye into the jaws of hell for her sake."

Tomas looked into his father's eyes. "I will, Da." It was a sobering thought.

Other than that brief moment of seriousness, Tomas spent the morning laughing and talking with his friends and family. It had been decided that Ethan would stay at Cotharach as Tomas's right hand. Drew too would stay for a while, but Tomas needed to discuss the long-term plans for that arrangement with Laird MacLennan. Niall also agreed to leave six of his men-at-arms at Cotharach for a while, to help build a strong garrison.

At last, just before noon, Beitris, Emma, and the servants who had been attending Vida entered the great hall and announced that she would be down in a few minutes. Tomas's father said, "That's yer cue. I'll wait for yer mother, but ye and Ethan should go now and wait in front of the chapel."

Tomas picked up the gift he had for Vida and left the keep. A jubilant crowd had formed, among them old friends, like Manus and Moyna, as well as new ones. All were waiting to celebrate the wedding. He thought back to the day his parents were married in the same chapel. He hadn't witnessed it. Lady Katherine had told him to wait for them outside the village. With everything turning upside down in her life, she had been worried about him. Tomas also thought about what his father had said about always putting Vida first and he understood why. She, like his mother, would always think of others. So, she needed one person who would always think of her. Between the two of them, the clan would be well served.

Father Michael met them at the steps of the chapel. "It's a bitter wind today, lads."

"Aye, Father, it is," said Ethan. "Maybe we could talk ye into moving this inside?"

"I'm sure God wouldn't mind," said the priest.

Tomas shook his head. "Nay, but Vida would. These are her people, she'll want them to witness our vows, and they all won't fit inside the chapel."

Father Michael nodded. "Aye, you're right about that. So, I'll do the next best thing."

"What's that?" asked Ethan.

Father grinned. "Talk fast."

All three men chuckled.

It wasn't long before a hush fell over the gathered crowd. Tomas looked toward the keep and saw his parents, his brothers, and Will descending the front steps and moving through the throng. Then his sister, who would be standing with Vida, left the keep, and the crowd parted for her. Finally, the doors opened for Vida and her father. She was so very beautiful, it took Tomas's breath away. He drank her in and didn't think he'd ever get his fill.

The fact that she was on the arm of a man he had once considered to be a monster no longer bothered him. Ambrose Ruthven was her father. He was flawed, and stubborn, and had a terrible temper. But he was also a loving father and in the end, he had chosen Vida's happiness and the good of the clan over his own wants. Tomas was willing now to leave the past where it belonged.

When they reached him, Father Michael asked, "Who gives this woman to be married to this man?"

Tears stood in Ambrose's eyes and his voice trembled a bit as he said, "I do." Then he leaned down, kissed Vida's cheek, and guided her gently to stand beside Tomas.

Tomas unfolded his gift, a length of thick warm plaid, made by MacIan weavers, and placed it around her shoulders. "I thought I told ye not to leave the keep without a wrap," he whispered and winked at her as in pinned it in place with a silver brooch resembling a ring of flowers.

"It's beautiful," she said fingering the brooch.

"The flowers are periwinkle. They're a symbol of Clan MacIan."

"Thank you, Tomas," she said.

"It's my promise to ye. I'll always protect ye, whether it be from a highwayman, an invading hoard, or a wee blustery winter wind."

He took her hand in his and turned to face the priest.

Father Michael had an amused look on his face. "That was a lovely promise, lad. Now I have a few more for ye to make before we can get in out of this *wee blustery wind*. So, Tomas MacIan, wilt thou have this woman to be thy wedded wife? Wilt thou love her, and honor her, keep her and guard her, in health and in sickness, as a husband should a wife, and forsaking all others on account of her, keep thee only unto her, so long as you both shall live?"

"I will," he answered.

"Davida Ruthven, will ye have this man to be thy wedded husband, will ye obey him, and serve him, love, honor, and keep him in sickness and in health; and, forsaking all others on account of him, keep ye only unto him, so long as ye both shall live?"

"I will," her voice sounded strong and clear in the chilly air.

"Is there a ring?" asked Father Michael.

Vida looked momentarily shocked. "N-nay Father. With everything…I…I forgot."

Tomas grinned. "But I didn't, Father. Turns out we do make a pretty good team."

"Aye, I'd say you do," said the priest, taking the simple gold rings from Tomas. He blessed them and gave one to Tomas who placed it on the third finger of Vida's left hand. "With this ring, I thee wed, in the name of the Father and the Son and the Holy Spirit."

Father gave the other ring to Vida who placed it on Tomas's left hand with the same words. Then Father blessed them and led them into the chapel, followed by all of the family and as many clansmen and women as would fit.

After saying Mass, Father gave them a final blessing, pronouncing them husband and wife. "You may kiss your bride."

Tomas cradled her face in his hands and kissed her gently. A resounding cheer went up and he whispered, "We'll continue this later."

She smiled, and to his delight, blushed.

"Are ye ready for our other announcement?" he asked, also in a whisper.

She nodded.

Tomas motioned to the crowd for silence and they obliged.

"Thank ye all for the joyous good wishes. We are honored and humbled. We would also like to take this opportunity to make one more announcement. We would not be here today had Will, the cabin boy on the *Mermaid Queen*, not been brave enough to travel back to Scotland and tell his tale, even though it meant impugning the honor of a nobleman. Will, we owe ye everything, and if ye're willing, we'd like to give ye a home here with us, just as the MacIans did for me."

The lad looked stunned. "You mean…as my parents?"

Vida laughed. "Aye, as your parents. Would you like that?"

"It's kind of a family tradition," added Tomas.

"Oh, aye, I'd like that a lot." He threw his arms around them both and another deafening cheer went up.

The entire assembly made their way to the keep where a great feast awaited them.

They partook of the wonderful food and danced through the afternoon and well into the evening.

At one point, when Vida and Tomas took a break from dancing and sat at the table with his parents, Uncle Ambrose approached them. He had been a bit subdued all day. He made his way to Katherine's side.

"Katherine, my dear, may I have a word?"

"Of course, Uncle."

He took one of her hands in his. "I have waited far too long for this. I am truly sorry for everything you suffered at my hands. I know you have heard the full story by now. I saw you only as an obstacle to my happiness and, honestly, I hated you for it. It was wrong and exceedingly unfair. I regret, with everything in me, the pain I caused you. And yet, I do not regret what I did to gain your title."

She smiled. "I don't either, Uncle. The MacIans were able to prosper as were the Ruthvens. I have been happier than you can imagine, married to Niall and having Tomas as a son."

He nodded. "I know you have. And I too found love and happiness, and was blessed with my precious daughter. I don't really have the right to ask this, but can you forgive me for the way it all happened?"

"Of course, I can Uncle. I forgave you long ago."

He leaned in and kissed her cheek. Then his brow furrowed. "You know, when I was just a lad, I overheard an old crone talking to someone. She caught my attention because she was toying with some sort of gold disk in her hands that was like nothing I'd ever seen. She said something I didn't quite understand at the time, but I always remembered it. She said, 'The universe unfolds as it should.' I think I understand that now. I was never meant to lead this clan. I don't have the skills it takes. It was only mine to steward for a while. And as hard as I worked against that fate, it was futile. You too were not intended to be Lady Ruthven for long. You had another destiny, and it was partially my own scheming that allowed you to find it. Still, you have left your mark here and you raised the man who *is* intended to lead Clan Ruthven into the future. Over the last few days, I have come to believe that the universe is, in fact, unfolding as it should and that sure knowledge has given me a peace that I have never known before."

Katherine smiled. "I think ye're right. What's meant to be has happened and we can either drag our heels or rejoice in it. I chose the latter years ago. I'm glad you feel the same way now." She leaned forward and kissed his cheek.

Tomas watched the entire exchange in amazement. Things had truly come full circle since that hot June day and everyone was the better for it. But the idea that he might have been destined for this left him in awe.

Vida reached out her hand to cover his where it rested on the table. He glanced towards her. Tears stood in her eyes. Clearly, she was as stunned as he. He turned his hand palm up, wrapping his fingers around hers and giving a squeeze.

His father cleared his throat. "I think it's time we bid this young couple goodnight and send them off to bed."

Murmurs of assent spread through the hall.

Before the crowd could take over and carry them both up to the bed chamber, Tomas stood and scooped Vida into his arms. "Father Michael, I need no further encouragement. Lead the way."

Father Michael nodded and headed toward the door. Tomas followed, carrying Vida. Then many of the assembled clansmen and women fell in behind them, calling out a range of bawdy suggestions.

When they reached Vida's chamber, Father blessed the bed and gave a final blessing to the couple for a long, happy, and fruitful marriage.

Then Tomas put his beautiful bride down and with Father's help, chivvied everyone out of the chamber.

Finally, he turned to Vida. "Well, my lovely lassie, ye're all mine now."

She laughed. "I've been all yours for days, weeks even."

"Aye, 'twas the same for me." He closed the distance between them and gathered her in his arms. "And I have been truly blessed."

He kissed her softly, then more insistently. When he broke the kiss, he fingered the brooch that still held his plaid around her shoulders. "As much as I love seeing ye wrapped in my plaid, I think it's time we removed it."

She grinned. "Oh, aye, it is. But now that you mention it, how did you get all of this? My plaid and brooch…and the rings?"

"When I sent the message asking for my parents help, I also asked for them to bring the plaid, brooch, and rings."

"You never feared that this might fall through?"

He laughed. "Nay, but you did. That's why we're so perfect together."

"Aye, I have to agree. Now, let's see if we can harness this perfection and create our legacy."

He gave a low throaty growl. "Oh, lass, ye needn't ask me twice."

EPILOGUE

June 22, 1380 (A year and a half later)

Tomas had left Cotharach nearly two weeks ago, traveling with Vida, their six-month-old son, Connall, and their adopted son, Will. They would be celebrating St. John's Eve with the MacIans, and staying for Beitris's wedding to Liam Sutherland in early July.

They had stopped at Castle Carr and visited for several days. After all, Connall had been named after Tomas's great-grandfather, who had been married to Laird Carr's great-aunt, Elasaid.

Then they'd travelled on to Brathanead, where they had visited with the MacLennans for nearly a week. Although not technically related by blood to the MacIans, Tomas considered Laird MacLennan to be his uncle.

At last they were approaching the southern tip of Loch Craos. In mere moments, they'd emerge from the forest and be able to see Duncurra, his parents' home.

When they passed the tree line, Vida exclaimed, "Oh, my, it certainly is an impressive fortress."

"It's built of stone and it's in the middle of the loch," said Will, astounded.

Tomas laughed, remembering he'd thought the same thing the first time he'd seen it. "It isn't actually, but it looks that way from here. Duncurra is built on a crag that juts into the loch. It's surrounded by water on three sides. You just can't see the tail of the crag from here. As we ride along the western edge of the loch, ye'll begin to see it."

Will cocked his head to one side. "That would make it much easier to defend wouldn't it?"

Will had turned out to be an extremely bright lad. He was eager to learn and mastered new skills quickly.

Normally, the sons of noblemen were sent to train with other clans when they were Will's age or a little older, but Tomas would break tradition on this. He liked Will and believed he had huge potential and wanted to train Will himself. So the lad would stay at Cotharach.

Tomas smiled. He hadn't been the only one to see Will's potential. Captain Lowther and the loyal members of his crew had returned to Scotland about a month after Tomas and Father Owen had arrived. As soon as the captain found out where Will had gone, he showed up at Cotharach. He said he was too old to go through another ordeal like this one, and was retiring from the sea. He had hoped to give the lad a home himself. But Captain Lowther agreed that life as the son of a nobleman would afford Will advantages that a retired sea captain couldn't.

However, Vida learned that the primary reason Captain Lowther left the sea was that a blow he'd received to his skull when the *Mermaid* was taken had left him with double vision and he suffered frequent headaches.

"Can't we adopt the captain too, Tomas?" Vida had asked.

"Vida, he's an old man. He doesn't need parents."

"You know what I mean. I want to offer him a home here with us. We owe it to him for making certain Will was saved from a life of slavery."

Of course, Tomas had agreed.

"Da, does it make Duncurra easier to defend?" asked Will again, drawing Tomas from his musings.

"Aye, Will, Duncurra is a much more impenetrable fortress than Cotharach. Well spotted. Duncurra and part of its village are surrounded by a wall, but only the front portion of it is manned. The crag provides natural protection. Can ye see the other advantage?"

"The castle is very high up. Like a crow's nest on a ship. They can probably already see us."

Tomas grinned. "Aye, that's right. From Duncurra's towers, anyone approaching can be seen at least an hour before they reach the castle, even if they are riding hard."

It took them closer to two hours to reach the castle. They moved a little more slowly because of the baby. A nursemaid, and sometimes Vida, rode with him in a cart.

By the time they reached Duncurra, the entire village had turned out to greet them as they had the first time Tomas had arrived with Lady Katherine so many years ago.

When they reached the castle, his parents and Beitris greeted them in the bailey.

His parents had travelled to Cotharach in November so that his mother, who was a healer and midwife, could attend Vida when she delivered Connall, but other than the Duncurra men who had ridden with them, this was the first time any of the rest of the clan had met Vida, Will, or the new baby.

Tomas had expected Turcuil's wife, Edna, and the other women who worked in the castle, to cluck and coo over the baby, but he had to chuckle at his father's men who did the same.

His father nudged him. "Ye know, nothing turns a man feeble-minded so quick as a bairn. If an attacking army arrived with a score or two of wee-ones, they could walk past all defenses."

Tomas laughed. "Nay, Da, they couldn't. They'd be just as smitten with the bairns themselves."

Niall nodded. "Aye, I suppose so. But it's why we do this, isn't it?"

"Why we do what?"

"We build fortresses and train guards. It's to protect that which we hold most dear. Our loved ones. Our wives and our children. If they weren't so precious, we'd have no need for any of this."

There was truth in his father's words. He had loved his family and clan and would have died to protect them. But now with a wife and children of his own, the need to keep them safe was infinitely stronger.

~ * ~

Vida had enjoyed the journey to Duncurra, with its lengthy stops to visit friends and family, but when they had finally arrived she could scarcely contain her excitement. This was the clan that had embraced her cousin as their lady and accepted a young peasant as their laird's son so many years ago. These people, along with Katherine and Niall had made Tomas into the man he was—the man she loved. Meeting them all and putting faces to the stories she had heard thrilled her.

If she thought they might be reserved or cool towards her, because of who her father was and what he had once done to their lady, she was wrong. She could not have been more warmly welcomed. They told story after story about Tomas as a lad, which had her laughing so hard her sides ached.

When they finally retired to their chamber that night and had tucked Connall into the cradle in which MacIan babies had slept for several generations, she was ready to sleep. She snuggled next to Tomas, his arms holding her securely.

"Are you glad to be home again?" she asked.

"Home?" he asked sleepily.

"Aye, Tomas. Are you glad to be at Duncurra again?"

"Aye, Duncurra is wonderful. It's good to see old friends again. But sweetling, Duncurra isn't my home."

"So, you consider Cotharach your home now?" The thought warmed her heart.

"Nay, my darling, Cotharach isn't my home either. At least, not always."

She frowned. "I don't understand. If you consider neither Cotharach nor Duncurra home, where is yer home?"

He chuckled. "My precious lass, my home is wherever ye are. If I can hold ye in my arms at the end of the day, I'm home."

ABOUT THE AUTHOR

Ceci started her career as an oncology nurse at a leading research hospital, and eventually became a successful medical writer. In 1991, she married a young Irish carpenter whom she met when his brother married her dear friend. They raised their family in central New Jersey but now live with their dogs and birds in paradise, also known as southwest Florida. Although still working occasionally as a consultant in the pharmaceutical industry, Ceci spends most of her time now writing "happily ever afters."

Follow Ceci at:

Website: www.cecigiltenan.com
Facebook: https://www.facebook.com/cgiltenan
Twitter: https://twitter.com/CeciGiltenan

**Don't miss the Duncurra YouTube channel -
https://www.youtube.com/duncurra!
You'll find videos of Scotland, Scottish words of
the day explained, free audiobooks, and much
more**

OTHER BOOKS BY CECI GILTENAN

If you enjoyed Highland Redemption, you may want to read the Duncurra series that started it all:

The Duncurra Series
(Available in e-book, paperback and audio)
Highland Solution

Laird Niall MacIan needs Lady Katherine Ruthven's dowry to relieve his clan's crushing debt, but he has no intention of giving her his heart in the bargain.

Niall MacIan, a Highland laird, desperately needs funds to save his impoverished clan. Lady Katherine Ruthven, a lowland heiress, is rumored to be "unmarriageable" and her uncle hopes to be granted her title and lands when the king sends her to a convent. King David II, anxious to strengthen his alliances, sees a solution that will give Ruthven the title he wants, and MacIan the money he needs. Laird MacIan will receive Lady Katherine's hand along with her substantial dowry and her uncle will receive her lands and title.

Lady Katherine must forfeit everything in exchange for a husband who does not want to be married and believes all women to be self-centered and deceitful. Can the lovely and gentle Katherine mend his heart and build a life with him or will he allow the treachery of others to destroy them?

Highland Courage

Her parents want a betrothal, but Mairead MacKenzie can't get married without revealing her secret and no man will wed her once he knows.

Plain in comparison to her siblings and extremely reserved, Mairead has been called "MacKenzie's Mouse" since she was a child. No one knows the reason for her timidity and she would just as soon keep it that way. When her parents arrange a betrothal to Laird Tadhg Matheson, she is horrified. She only sees one way to prevent an old secret from becoming a new scandal.

Tadhg Matheson admires and respects the MacKenzies. While an alliance with them through marriage to Mairead would be in his clan's best interest, he knows Laird MacKenzie seeks a closer alliance with another clan. When Tadhg learns of her terrible shyness and her youngest brother's fears about her, Tadhg offers for her anyway.

Secrets always have a way of revealing themselves. With Tadhg's unconditional love, can Mairead find the strength and courage she needs to handle the consequences when they do?

Highland Intrigue

Lady Gillian MacLennan's clan needs a leader, but the last person on earth she wants as their laird is Fingal MacIan. She can neither forgive nor forget that his mother killed her father, and, by doing so, created Clan MacLennan's current desperate circumstances.

King David knows a weak clan, without a laird, can change quickly from a simple annoyance to a dangerous liability, and he cannot ignore the turmoil. The MacIan's owe him a great debt, so when he makes Fingal MacIan laird of clan MacLennan and requires that he marry Lady Gillian, Fingal is in no position to refuse.

In spite of the challenge, Fingal is confident he can rebuild her clan, ease her heartache, and win her affection. However, just as love awakens, the power struggle takes a deadly turn. Can he protect her from the unknown long enough to uncover the plot against them? Or will all be lost, destroying the happiness they seek in each other's arms?

Pocket Watch Chronicles

The Pocket Watch

When Maggie Mitchell is transported to the thirteenth century Highlands, will Laird Logan Carr help mend her broken heart or put it in more danger than before?

Generous, kind, and loving, Maggie nearly always puts the needs of others first. So when a mysterious elderly woman gives her an extraordinary pocket watch, telling her it's a conduit to the past, Maggie agrees to give the watch a try, if only to disprove the woman's delusion.

But it works.

Maggie finds herself in the thirteenth-century Scottish Highlands with a handsome warrior who clearly despises her. Her tender soul is caught between her own desire and the disaster she could cause for others. Will she find a way to resolve the trouble and return home within the allotted sixty days? Or will someone worthy earn her heart forever?

The Midwife

Can a twenty-first century independent woman find her true destiny in thirteenth-century Scotland?

At his father's bidding, Cade MacKenzie begs a favor from Laird Macrae—Lady MacKenzie desperately needs the renowned Macrae midwife. Laird Macrae has no intention of sending his clan's best, instead he passes off Elsie, a young woman with little experience, as the midwife they seek.

But fate—in the form of a mysterious older woman and an extraordinary pocket watch—steps in.

Elizabeth Quinn, a disillusioned obstetrician, is transported to the thirteenth century. She switched souls with Elsie as the old woman said she would, but other things don't go quite as expected. Perhaps most unexpected was falling in love.

Once Found

Elsie thought she had found love.

The handsome young minstrel awoke her desire and his music fed her soul. But just as love was blossoming, the inconceivable happened—Elsie awoke more than seven hundred years in the future, in the body of Dr. Elizabeth Quinn.

Gabriel Soldani thought he had found love several times, only to have it slip from his grasp. In medical school, he had fallen hard for Elizabeth Quinn, but their careers led them in different directions. When their paths cross again, he hopes they've been given another chance.

There's only one problem…the woman he's never forgotten doesn't remember him.

Once love is found…and then lost…can it be found again?

The Christmas Present

A Pocket Watch Novella

Faced with an empty nest, and heartbroken, Anita Lewis is given the chance to experience Christmas in another time with the help of a mysterious old woman and a pocket watch.

The gift she receives is priceless as she rediscovers the magic of Christmas in the past.

The Choice

The Choice contains 2, brand-new, full-length novels, each with a different HEA.

Sixty days in another life, another time…it's tempting. Now the decision to accept the pocket watch is yours. What choice will you make?

Sara Wells is in Venice, preparing to leave on a fourteen day cruise to Greece, when Gertrude offers her the pocket watch.

Will she take it? You choose.

If you accept the watch, Sara will travel to eighteenth century Venice where she meets a young Scottish expatriate who owns a small ship building company. Will their love for each other be enough to overcome all obstacles?

If you refuse the watch, Sara will remain in the twenty-first century, where she will encounter a traveler from the past and more intrigue than she can pack into the books she writes.

Once you've read one, you can go back and make the other choice.

One choice, two souls, two different happy endings.

The Fated Hearts Series
(Available in e-book, paperback and audio)

Highland Revenge

Does he hate her clan enough to visit his vengeance on her? Or will he listen to her secret and his own heart's yearning?

Hatred lives and breathes between medieval clans who often don't remember why feuds began in the shadowed past.

But Eoin MacKay remembers.

He will never forget how he was treated by Bhaltair MacNicol—the acting head of Clan MacNicol. He was lucky to escape alive, and vows to have revenge.

Years later, as laird of Clan MacKay, he gets his chance when he captures Lady Fiona MacNicol. His desire for revenge is strong but he is beguiled by his captive.

Can he forget his stubborn hatred long enough to listen to the secret she has kept for so long? And once he knows the truth, can he show her she is not alone and forsaken? In the end, is he strong enough to fight the combined hostilities and age-old grudges that demand he give her up?

Highland Echoes

Love echoes.

Grace Breive is strong and independent because she has to be. She has a wee daughter to care for and, having lost her parents and husband, has no one else on whom she can rely. Driven from the only home she has ever known, she travels to Castle Sutherland to find a grandmother she never knew she had.

As Laird Sutherland's heir, Bram Sutherland understands his obligation to enter into a political marriage for the good of the clan, but he is captivated by the beautiful and resilient young mother.

Will Bram and Grace follow the dictates of their hearts, or will echoes from the past force them apart?

Highland Angels

Anna MacKay fears the MacLeods. Andrew MacLeod fears love.

Anna, angry with her brother, took a walk to cool her temper. She had no intention of venturing so close to MacLeod territory—until she saw a wee lad fall through the ice.

Andrew becomes enraged when it appears the MacKay lass has abducted his son, his last precious connection to the wife he lost—until he learns the truth. Anna risked her life to save his beloved child.

Now there is a chance to end the generations old hate and fear between their clans.

Fate connects them. The desire for peace binds them. Will a rival tear them apart?

ABOUT DUNCURRA

Duncurra is a small independent publishing company. We highly value the heart and soul, energy, time, and talent that our authors pour into their stories. Unlike many independent publishers, we help authors build their readership by investing significantly in marketing platforms to complement the author's own promotional efforts.

We are particularly proud of our YouTube presence and ever increasing subscribership there, which is unique to the publishing industry.

Whether you are a reader, an established author, or an aspiring author, we have a lot to offer. We take the reader experience to a new level, connecting authors and readers in unprecedented ways.

Visit our website at www.duncurra.com.

To stay up to date on all Duncurra releases, sales, giveaways, and more. Sign up for our newsletter here on our website.

Experience the difference.

Experience Duncurra!

Award Winning, New York Times Bestselling Author

Kathryn Lynn Davis

Highland Awakening

Can the transforming power of magic help two people on a perilous journey create a miracle—even when one of them doesn't believe?

Since she lost her brother and nearly her father, Esmé Rose fears the world beyond her family and her garden. But one year when winter clings overlong, a dream begins to haunt her, forcing her to take a journey and face a challenge more difficult than she could ever imagine.

Magnus MacLeod is a skilled healer, always curious to know more. He, too, is called by a dream he doesn't quite believe in, despite its physical effects on him. He and Esmé travel a treacherous road that takes them to a magical place. There they must put aside their feelings for one another—and their difference in beliefs—long enough to make a miracle.

Sing to Me of Dreams

One woman's journey of discovery…through all the mysteries of the human heart.

As a child, Saylah held the magic and wisdom of her Salish Indian people. But when tragedy ravages the Salish, she must leave them for the world of the Ivys – an English/Scottish family whose traditions are as strange to her as her spirit world is to them. The Ivys have come to fertile British Columbia in search of paradise, but the secrets and mysteries surrounding them are overwhelming – until Saylah comes to help them understand the darkness holding them back.

Frustrated Julian Ivy, in whom sophistication and fury entwine, is drawn to Saylah's healing strength and disquieting beauty. Through sorrow and elation, the two discover the fullness of love...but no one can resolve for her the contradictions of her birthright. Following the songs of her heritage, she will finally make the most wrenching choice of all...

Weave for Me a Dream

The long awaited sequel to Sing to Me of Dreams!

Saylah's journey continues as secrets woven in the past threaten the fabric of her family.

Victoria, Vancouver Island, B.C.

1895

Saylah Ivy, once shaman of her Salish tribe, now wife and mother, continues her journey of discovery, following her white husband Julian as he seeks new adventure in the city.

Where Saylah and their daughter Illiann must meet the challenge of living two lives: both Salish and White, while facing prejudice, discovery and danger along the way. Julian and their son Kit confront a powerful enemy who threatens their very lives. Meanwhile, secrets from their pasts haunt them daily.

The family must protect themselves from threats to both their bodies and their souls. They must battle their enemies to stay true to who they have become, and to discover a place where their hearts are at peace. Perhaps hardest of all, they must find a way to forgive those who hurt them long ago.

Award Winning, Bestselling Author
Lily Baldwin
Highland Outlaw Series

(All of the Highland Outlaw series are complete standalone stories and can be read in any order.)

Jack: A Scottish Outlaw

Freedom is not won…it is stolen

Jack MacVie and his brother are thieves, robbing English nobles on the road north into Scotland. They're about to attack the Redesdale carriage when another band of villains, after more than Lady Redesdale's coin, sweeps down and steals their prize. Despite his hatred for the English, Jack's conscience forces him to kidnap the lady to save her life.

In the aftermath of the Berwick massacre, Lady Isabella Redesdale's world is shattered. Her mother is dead, her father lost to grief, and she's risking it all, journeying north into war-torn Scotland to be with her sister.

Although they come from different worlds, Jack and Isabella are more alike than they first realize. They both crave freedom from war and despair, but in a world where kings reign and birth dictates one's station, freedom is not won, it is stolen.

Quinn: A Scottish Outlaw

He is an outlaw…And the only man she can trust.

Quinn MacVie is in pursuit of a prize, but it is unlike any plunder he has stolen before. He seeks neither gold nor jewels, but something infinitely more valuable—Lady Catarina Ravensworth. Sent by the lady's sister, who fears Catarina is in danger, Quinn's mission is to steal the lady away from Ravensworth castle. But nothing there is as Quinn expected.

Lady Catarina has been accused of a horrific crime and is forced to run or face a fate worse than death.

But she is not alone.

Thief and Scottish rebel, Quinn MacVie, is at her side. With a price on her head, they must disappear into the wilds of the Scottish Highlands where the only thing greater than the danger following at their heels is the desire burning in their hearts.

Rory: A Scottish Outlaw

Lady Alexandria MacKenzie is one of Abbot Matthew's network of rebels, fighting for Scottish independence. When her father dies, leaving their clan without a laird, she asks the abbot for aid in finding a husband. He sends her a selection of three noblemen from which to choose. Accompanying them is secret agent and reputed rake, Rory MacVie, who must assist Alexandria with a perilous mission for Scotland. But the abbot makes one point very clear--Rory is not a potential suitor.

This is a passionate story of honor, rebellion, and forbidden love.

Alec: A Scottish Outlaw

Two broken hearts unite, becoming one love that will last forever.

Sold from one ruthless master to another, Joanie is a servant who has lived her whole life in fear. When Randolph Tweed, an English merchant with cold, unfeeling eyes, buys her, she fears she has fallen into the hands of her cruelest master yet. But what she doesn't realize is that Randolph is actually Alec MacVie, Scottish spy and rebel.

The first time Alec sees Joanie is in his dreams. He has a vision of a young woman standing on a bridge alone, bleeding, and broken hearted. He must rescue her, and when he does he soon realizes she holds the power to rescue him right back.

Join Alec and Joanie on a journey of healing, passion, and hope, where their love and strength forge a new destiny for themselves and for Scotland.

Stephanie Joyce Cole

Compass North

Can you ever run away from your own life?

Reeling from the shock of a suddenly shattered marriage, Meredith flees as far from her home in Florida as she can get without a passport: to Alaska.

After a freak accident leaves her presumed dead, she stumbles into a new identity and a new life in a quirky small town. Her friendship with a fiery and temperamental artist and her growing worry for her elderly, cranky landlady pull at the fabric of her carefully guarded secret. When a romance with a local fisherman unexpectedly blossoms, Meredith struggles to find a way to meld her past and present so that she can move into the future she craves. But someone is looking for her, someone who will threaten Meredith's dream of a reinvented life.

James Donbar

Pacificus

What happens when a group of the world's wealthiest people desire a haven for themselves and their assets?

Pacificus is built one hundred miles off the coast of Ecuador. This manmade island is governed solely by a set of principles and relies on the common sense of its inhabitants instead of laws.

What could go wrong?

For Gaspar Delgado, the island's administrator, nothing. He need only find the balance between the privileged indulgence of its residents and order.

However, Conrad Silverstein, a smug self-serving newspaper editor, is certain something sinister lurks under the high-minded values supposedly espoused by Pacificans and sends reporter, Alicia Jones, to find out what it is.

Will this utopia be threatened by those willing to exploit liberty at any expense?

Ford Murphy

Taking the Town

Lissadown, Ireland 1986.

A ruthless, violent criminal gang has held the small midlands town in its grip for too long.

Innocents have been maimed, raped, killed.

Law enforcement is paralyzed.

Finn Lane has had enough. A newcomer to Lissadown and an expert MMA fighter, Finn can't be intimidated. Keeping his head down and minding his own business is not an option. The gang may think they own the town and everyone in it but those days are coming to an end.

He will have vengeance...

MJ Platt

Somewhere Montana

*Can Callum "Mac" Maclain make Sage Burnett believe in his love for her and
save her from her stalker?*

Escaping from a stalker, Sage Burnett crashes her plane on a mountain, part of the ranch owned by the man who rejected her eight years ago. She still loves him and prays he isn't around because she dreads facing him to only have him reject her again.

Callum "Mac" MacLain, the ranch owner, a Marine home on medical leave rescues her from the mountain. He persuades her to stay until she heals. He realizes he is still in love with her. Can he save her from her stalker and convince her his love is real?

B.J. Scott

Talisman of Light

Will changing the Past destroy their future?

Intent on setting a wrong to right, Alex Innes flies to Scotland to return an Ancient Talisman to its rightful resting place. But his plane crashes and he finds himself in twelfth century Scotland, where winter holds the country in its icy grip and only one maiden can set it free. Ciara Dunmore offers her life to appease the winter hag on the Imbolc Festival, but Alex has different plans for the beguiling lass who has captured his heart. Will changing the past destroy their future?

Forever and Beyond

Katherine MacDonald trades her luxury Manhattan apartment, high paying job, and abusive fiancé for what she believes is a rundown estate, deep in the Scottish Highlands, unaware that her future, and perhaps her very life, depends on secrets deeply rooted in the past.

When she discovers a ring with a sentimental inscription and a journal written by one of her ancestors within the ancient croft, she suddenly finds herself in fourteenth century Scotland where she comes face to face with Ayden MacAndrews, a braw Highlander who has haunted her dreams since she was a child.

Will Katherine and Ayden be able to right an ancient wrong? Will their love stand the test of time?

Jennifer Siddoway

Dealing with the Devil

Wynnona Hendricks has some shocking surprises in store. Struggling to figure out her comatose mother's secret, Wynn gets more than she bargained for, and ends up caught between the realms of Heaven, Hell, and Earth, fighting for her life.

Family and friends are stunned by her bizarre behavior; the only one who believes in her is Caleb, an angel who chose to spare her life. But by saving her, he may have started a war between the factions, throwing the Mortal Realm into mayhem. Wynn discovers new allies, new enemies—including her own human weakness—and new powers as she fights to protect her family from being ripped apart.

The Devil's Due

After tragedy strikes the Hendricks family, Wynn leaves for college, hoping the Demon Lords follow her. She is reunited with Caleb after his fall from grace. Now, they no longer have to hide their feelings for one another. Together, they prepare for Wynn's three remaining trials and encounter another demon who has infiltrated the Mortal Realm.

Charlene is strong and beautiful, with complete control of her demonic powers – everything Wynn hopes to achieve one day. She learns that to defeat Aidan once and for all will come at a terrible price, taking her away from the ones that she loves most. The Demon Lords aren't holding back, but they're not the only ones who are conspiring against her. Maya is on the war path and blames Wynn for Caleb's decision to leave.

With the help of some unlikely allies, can Wynn defeat the Demon Lords and finally make Aidan pay?

www.ingramcontent.com/pod-product-compliance
Lightning Source LLC
Chambersburg PA
CBHW031725170626
46808CB00005B/1899